ISABELLE

Crystal River Book Two

JESSICA AIKEN-HALL

MOONLIT MADNESS
PRESS

Copyright © 2021 Jessica Aiken-Hall

First Edition.

All rights reserved. No part of this publication may be reproduced, stored in any retrieval system, or transmitted, in any form or by any means, electronic, mechanical, photocopying, recording or otherwise, without the prior written permission of the author. If you would like permission to use material from the book (other than for review purposes), please contact http://jessicaaikenhall.com/contact

This is a work of fiction. Names, characters, businesses, organizations, products, places, and events portrayed in this novel are either products of the author's imagination or used fictitiously. Any resemblance to actual persons, living or dead, events or locales is entirely coincidental.

ISBN-13: 978-1-9550710-5-5 (paper)

Library of Congress Control Number: 2021918639

Moonlit Madness Press

Cover Design © Indigo Hearts Designs

Editor: Maria Vickers

*Warning- Contains sensitive subject matter including, but not limited to sexual abuse.

jessicaaikenhall.com

For my daughter, Alana.

ALSO BY JESSICA AIKEN-HALL

Demi: Crystal River Book One

Boundaries: Scope of Practice Book One

Confidentiality: Scope of Practice Book Two

Accountability: Scope of Practice Book Three

Rebecca Remains: Shadow of a Doubt Book One

Murder at Honeybee Lake: Shadow of a Doubt Book Two

House in the Woods

Reclaim Your Power: Heal Trauma by Telling Your Story

The Monster That Ate My Mommy- A Memoir

CHAPTER ONE

The silk bathrobe fell to the floor as the moonlight illuminated the room. I crawled into bed and snuggled close to Richard, kissing his neck. "Want to fool around?" I whispered before I nibbled on his ear.

He reached over and kissed me, caressing my breast with his warm, muscular hand. "We've got to be quick; she's in the shower." He slipped out of his boxers and pressed his body into mine.

The heat from his body on top of mine made me crave more than he could give me. I needed Richard to be mine. I didn't want to share with Elizabeth or anyone else. Our bodies collided together like waves splashing onto the beach. Together, we were just as dangerous as the power of water. We were an untamed force of nature.

His lips lingered on mine before he rolled off me.

"She just turned the water off. You've got to get out of here." Richard slid his boxers back on.

"No, I don't want to leave." I folded my arms and kicked my feet. "Who cares if she finds us."

"Come on, don't be like that. You know she'll kick me out if she finds out." He leaned over and gave me one last kiss. "You don't want to lose me, do you?" He brushed the hair out of my eyes.

"No." I sighed as I pushed the covers off. "I wasn't done with you."

Richard smiled as he pulled the blanket up. "There's always tomorrow."

I tied my robe shut and went back to my room. After I slid into my sweatpants, I laid on my bed and let the sensations from my time with Richard tingle my senses. The more I was supposed to stay away from him, the more I wanted him. The desire washed away everything else I thought I knew. When he wasn't touching me, all I could think about was the next time his hands would be on my body.

I ran my fingertips over my lips and closed my eyes, imagining it was his touch I felt. Instead, she was in his bed. She was the one who got to fall asleep in his arms. Jealousy surged through my body. It wasn't fair that she got him, and I didn't. He didn't love her. He couldn't. I knew in my heart he wanted to be with me.

I went to my door and listened. The sound of my heartbeat echoed in my ears as I tried to hear what they were doing. I cracked my door to see if I could figure out what was going on. It was quiet. Too quiet. I didn't like what that could mean. I closed my door and paced my room, biting at my fingernail.

When I couldn't take the unknown any longer, I left my room and went to theirs. I opened the door and scanned the area. Richard and Elizabeth were in bed, next to each other. I pushed out a cough. "I don't feel good." I covered my mouth and coughed louder. "I said, I don't feel good. I think I need to go to the hospital."

"What's wrong?" Elizabeth sat up and turned on her lamp. "Do you have a fever?" She jumped out of bed, her flimsy nightgown exposing her breasts.

I swatted her hand off my forehead. "Get off me and go put on some clothes." I rolled my eyes and crossed my arms.

"What's wrong? You said you don't feel well." Elizabeth reached for her robe and covered herself. "Is everything okay?"

"No, it's not okay. I told you I don't feel good. I need some medicine or something." I scowled as I looked in at Richard.

"What's wrong?" Elizabeth frowned as she took a step closer to me.

"I said I don't feel good. God." I rolled my eyes. "Can I get something to help with the pain?"

"Where are you having pain?" The softness of Elizabeth's voice sent shock waves of rage throughout my body.

"Why does it matter? Just give me some goddamn

pills." I folded my arms and waited for her to jump to my demand. "Well, are you going to get them, or am I going to stand here and die?"

"I can't just give you pills without knowing what's going on. Maybe you need to go to the hospital. You seem upset." She took a step closer to me.

"I don't need to go anywhere. You need to go get me some pills."

"Why don't you go back to bed?" Richard joined us in the doorway.

"Excuse me? That's not what you were saying a few minutes ago." My smile grew as I stared him in the eyes.

"What are you talking about?" Richard wrapped his arm around Elizabeth. "Come on, honey, let's go back to bed."

"No, wait. What are you talking about?" Elizabeth reached for my hand. "Is everything alright?"

"Never mind. I'm fine. Why don't you go back to bed and leave me the hell alone?" I stormed down the hall to my bedroom and slammed the door behind me.

Elizabeth followed me and attempted to open the door. I held my body against it so she couldn't get in. "What's going on? Are you alright? Do you want to go to the hospital?"

"Jesus, I said I was fine. Now leave me alone."

"I'm worried about you. You're not acting like yourself. Can I please come in?" Elizabeth turned the doorknob.

"No, I'm fine. Just go back to bed."

"Are you sure?"

"Yes, now leave me alone." I slid to the floor, my back against the door, and buried my head in my knees. She'd never understand that she was my problem. Life would be so much better without her.

CHAPTER TWO

I slipped out of the house for school before anyone saw me. I wasn't ready to talk about what happened last night. A swishing sound happened with every step. When I was out of sight of the house, I stopped and unzipped my backpack. A bottle of vodka tucked under my folders was the culprit. I opened the bottle and sniffed the contents. "Oh my god. Where in the world did this come from?" I dumped the liquid into the grass, looking around to make sure no one was watching.

I tossed the empty bottle under the bush and brushed my hands off on my pants. Elizabeth was probably trying to set me up. It would be just like her to call the school and tell them to search me to watch me get in trouble. I can't wait until I could save up enough money to move out and get my own place. I didn't need roommates like them, at least not like her. I could deal with Richard. I knew that was what he wanted too.

"Hey, wait up." The high-pitched voice caught me off guard.

"Hi." I pushed the hair behind my ear. "Did you get the reading done last night?"

"Yeah, it took me all night." Kendra put her arm around my back. "Did you?"

"No, I think I fell asleep. It was too much. I don't know how you managed to get it done." I leaned into Kendra. "Tell me what happened?"

"I read it. I didn't say I remember what I read." She laughed as she pulled her arm away. "Sit next to me in case we have a quiz. I'll make sure you can see the answers."

"You're a lifesaver. I'll read tonight; you can take the night off." I tightened the grip on the strap of my backpack. "I can't wait for summer. This year has been brutal."

"I know, but then we won't be together." Kendra hung her head. "I'm going to miss you so much."

"Me too, but it'll only be a few years. Maybe you'll find some hot guys to hook up with." I waggled my eyebrows.

"Oh my god, is that all you think about?" Kendra shook her head. "You're impossible."

I shrugged. "Hey, why not make the best of it?"

"You're too much." Kendra snorted. "I guess you'll

have to come visit me. You can have your pick of the litter."

"Pick of the litter? I'm not getting a puppy."

"It might be easier. Puppies don't break your heart or cheat on you."

"Okay, okay, enough of this. Shake it off. Let's enjoy these last few weeks together. We can figure it all out later." I took Kendra's hand and gave it a squeeze.

"Do you want to come over after school?"

"Yeah, maybe. That would be nice." Hand in hand, we walked into Crystal River High School. "Let's make every moment count, okay?"

"Deal." Kendra gave my hand a tug.

We went our separate ways to get to class. "See you in English." I gave her a wave before I turned to enter my classroom.

I found my seat in the back of the room and took out my history book. "Isabelle loves Richard" was scrawled all over the book cover. My face heated at the sight of my juvenile artwork. I tore the paper bag cover off my book and crumpled it up, shoving it into my backpack.

I felt a tap on my shoulder. When I turned around, Marcus raised his eyebrows. "Hey, you owe me."

"Owe you what?" The kink in my neck pulled my attention away before his answer.

"You know. Don't be a tease, Izzy."

"It's Isabelle." I pushed my dark hair off my shoulder and spun around to make eye contact with him.

"Yeah, sure it is, whatever you say." Marcus rolled his eyes. "Just don't make promises you can't keep."

"I have no idea what you're talking about." I squinted my eyes as I tried to recall what he was talking about.

"Today, after school, meet me in the parking lot. I've got my mom's minivan today." He pushed his tongue into his cheek and smiled.

"Oh, you think I want to do that to you?" I scrunched up my nose.

"You didn't complain last time." Marcus opened his book and looked down.

"You must be mistaken." I spun back around in my seat.

The tap on my shoulder returned. Marcus held his phone out for me to see a photo of my head in his lap. I covered my mouth. "You didn't have a lot to say, but it was a good time." He turned his phone off before placing it on his desk.

The pain settled into my head as I tried to recall the image Marcus had shown me. Last night's dinner pushed its way into my throat. I covered my mouth and rushed to the bathroom. I pushed the stall door open and let loose. What was happening to me? After I flushed the remnants of my shame away, I sat on the toilet and sobbed. I closed my eyes and tried to telepathically get Kendra to join me. As I expected, it didn't work. I pulled my feet up and hugged my legs as I rocked.

The bathroom door swung open, and the room filled

with cigarette smoke. "Who's in here?" A bang on the metal door forced my eyes to close tighter, trying to make myself invisible. "I said, who's in here?"

"It's just me." I managed to get the words out between the tears.

"Me? Who's me?" The voice on the other side of the door mocked me.

"It's Isabelle. Don't worry, I won't tell anyone you're in here." I wiped my nose on a balled-up clump of toilet paper.

"I don't give a damn who you tell. What are you doing in here, anyway?"

"Just needed to take a break." I sniffled, filling my nose with smoke. I pushed it out as fast as I had inhaled it.

"I'm Bertha. My mom had the great idea to move us to this shithole town a month before summer vacation." Her cigarette butt sizzled as she extinguished it in the sink.

"Hi, Bertha. It's nice to meet you." I opened the door and held out my hand.

She laughed and crossed her arms. "Yeah, I don't do that touchy-feely shit. I just need to get through these last few weeks."

"I hear you. I can't wait to get out of here either." I washed my hands, watching Bertha in the mirror.

"Why were you crying?" Bertha leaned against the wall.

"Just stupid stuff. It's nothing." I tossed the paper towel into the trash. "See you around."

"Yeah, maybe." Bertha shrugged and walked out of the bathroom. I tried to see which classroom she went into, but I lost sight of her. I couldn't tell if we were going to be friends or if I should stay away from her. I wasn't sure which would be better.

CHAPTER THREE

My heart fluttered when I didn't see Elizabeth's car when I arrived home. I brushed the hair out of my face and licked my lips before I opened the door. "Honey, I'm home." I giggled as I stepped into the kitchen.

"Oh, hi there. I'm glad you're feeling better." Elizabeth's smile was like gasoline on a fire, igniting my fury.

"What are *you* doing here?" I glared at her with narrowed eyes.

"What do you mean? I live here." Elizabeth laughed as she put the dishes in the cupboard.

"Where's your car? Why aren't you at work?" I crossed my eyes and bit the inside of my cheek.

"Richard has my car. He's getting my oil changed, and I called out of work today." She turned around to look at me, leaning against the counter. "I'm worried about you, honey."

"Jesus Christ. Book me an intervention." I stormed down the hall to my room.

"Why are you so angry with me lately? We used to be such good friends." Elizabeth followed behind me.

"We were never friends. You're delusional. Maybe you should worry about your damn self. Leave me alone. I can take care of myself." I slammed the door in her face.

"What did I do to you to make you treat me like this?" Elizabeth's defeated voice made my skin crawl.

I sprawled out on my bed and sent Kevin a text. "Hey, what are you up to?"

"Work." A sad face followed his answer.

"I need to get out of here." I pushed the tears off my cheek. "Come get me?"

"I get out in an hour. I'll see you then."

I rested my eyes and imagined life with Kevin. It wasn't what I wanted, but it would do for now. I needed a man, not a boy. It felt like I was wasting my time with him, but at least he wanted to be with me all the time. I was only what Richard wanted when it was convenient for him.

I sat in front of my vanity and looked into my eyes. I was worth more than being someone's second choice. I brushed the blush onto my cheeks and touched up my mascara. Maybe Kevin wasn't such a bad option after all. I unbuttoned the top two buttons of my shirt and adjusted my bra. I needed more. With a couple more buttons undone, it was perfect. I smiled at the reflection in the mirror. "This will work."

The incoming text pulled my attention away from myself. "I'm here."

I pushed the curtains back and saw the Dodge pulled up in front of the house before rushing out my door. "Where are you going?" Elizabeth's hands were in the soapy water at the kitchen sink.

"Out."

"When will you be home? Should I save dinner for you?" She dried her hands off on the towel hanging by the sink.

"Don't bother." The front door closed behind me, and I raced to Kevin's car.

"Wow, you look hot." Kevin leaned in to kiss me.

I held his face with my hands and kissed him, licking his lips before putting my tongue in his mouth. "Let's go somewhere private." I placed my hand on his thigh and rubbed up his leg.

"Whoa, really? You want to do that?" His eyes widened.

I reached over and nibbled on his ear. "I do. Let's go." The breath from my whisper gave him goosebumps.

"Well, I wasn't expecting this." Kevin cleared his throat. "My parents are probably going to be gone for a while longer if you want to go back to my place."

"What about Kendra?" I tightened my grip on his leg and licked my lips.

"She's probably in her room. She'll never see us."

"Okay, let's go." I took his hand and sucked on his index finger.

"Holy shit, what's gotten into you?" Kevin blinked his eyes.

"I want you to make love to me. I need you."

"Oh my god, you're so hot." Kevin pulled his hand away and shook it. "I can't believe this is happening."

I unhooked my bra and pulled it out of my sleeve, letting the air hit my breasts.

"Holy shit." Kevin reached his hand over to cover my chest. "People are going to see." I held his hand on my skin and inched closer to him.

"I need you, Kevin."

"We're almost there." Kevin glanced at me and then back at the road. "What's gotten into you?" He shook his head. "Whatever it is, I like it."

I pushed out my chest with his hand still on my breast and let his skin rub against my nipple. "I want to feel you inside of me." I bit my lip and looked at him as he pulled his hand away to put the car in park.

Kevin leaned over and rubbed my breast as he kissed me. "Oh my god. I want to be inside you so bad." I let my tongue linger on his lips, and he pulled away to get out of the car. "Come on, let's get inside."

I got out of the car and followed him to his bedroom. My clothes hit the floor before he closed the door. When Kevin walked over to me, I unbuttoned his jeans as he pulled off his shirt. He kicked off his pants and guided me to his bed. We laid together, our bodies intertwined as we made love.

With every thrust inside, I felt more powerful. I had him right where I wanted him. I could make him do anything I wanted him to. I let pleasure take over my thoughts as our connection deepened. With every touch, I felt more alive. This was how it was supposed to be.

CHAPTER FOUR

I needed more of the power I felt with Kevin. Richard was an easy option. We slept in the same house every night. I simply needed to make him want me as much as I wanted him. After my shower, I left the bathroom with just a towel wrapped around my body. I looked down the hall and saw Richard in the living room watching TV. Elizabeth wasn't around.

I went into the living room and adjusted my towel enough that Richard could see my breasts. Water dripped off my hair onto my skin. I bit my bottom lip and looked him up and down, placing my fingers on my chest. I ran them around the outline of my breast and walked to my room. I sat on my bed and waited for my door to open.

My heart pounded with excitement when I heard footsteps getting closer. I arched my back and let the towel fall. Richard came in, locking the door behind him.

"What are you trying to do? Get me into trouble?" He pulled off his sweatpants and got on top of me.

"I need you." I bit his neck.

"Don't do that. She'll see." Richard pulled away from me.

"Don't stop." I jerked him closer, guiding him back on top of me. I closed my eyes and let everything disappear, only feeling the pleasure he was giving me. He rolled off me before getting up and pulling his pants back on and leaving.

Alone in my bed, I curled into a ball and sobbed. I wanted more. I needed more. Everything felt right with Richard, even better than with Kevin. I slipped on my pajamas and went out to the living room. Elizabeth and Richard were sitting on the couch together watching the news. I wedged myself between the two of them and sat down.

"Could you push over a little?" I turned to look at Elizabeth and smiled.

"Yeah, sure." Elizabeth moved the throw pillows to the floor and pushed over to the other end of the sofa. "Is that good, honey?" She reached for my hair.

"Yeah, it's great." I swatted her hand away.

"It's so nice of you to join us. We were just about to find something to watch." She handed me the remote. "Here, why don't you pick something."

"No thanks." I smiled as I leaned back and crossed my legs.

"What are you doing?" Richard raised his eyebrows.

"Watching TV. What are you doing?" I pushed my smile up.

"You could clearly see we were sitting here together. What are you doing?" Richard rubbed his chin.

"It's okay." Elizabeth leaned forward to look past me.

"No, it's not. It's rude." Richard crossed his arms. "She's just trying to make us fight. Can't you see that?"

"I think it's nice she wants to spend time with us." Elizabeth smiled and tapped my knee. "It's nice to have you out here with us."

"Jesus Christ, I can't believe you can't see what she's trying to do." Richard got up and stormed out of the room. "I'm going for a drive. I can't take this shit."

"What's his problem?" I pulled my feet under me and stretched out into the spot he vacated.

"Oh, I don't know why he's upset." Elizabeth put her hand on my leg. "I'm sure he'll be back soon."

"Why do you care?" I twirled a strand of hair around my finger. "He's kind of a jerk, isn't he?"

"No, he's a good man. You know that. He'd do anything for us."

"Do you think he's going to his girlfriend's house?" I scrunched up my nose. "What if he's having sex with her right now?"

"He wouldn't do that. He's not like that." Elizabeth smiled. "You don't have anything to worry about."

"I'm not worried, but you should be."

"Why do you say that?" Elizabeth picked at the thread on the cushion.

"What would you do if you found out he had a girlfriend? Would you stay with him?"

"I don't know. No, of course not. But he wouldn't do that to me. I know he loves me." Elizabeth bit her fingernail.

"You never know. People aren't always who they seem." I shrugged.

"Do you know something you're not telling me?" Elizabeth looked away and blinked before glancing back at me. "Is he having an affair?"

I lifted my shoulders.

"If you know something, please tell me." Elizabeth lowered her head. "I guess he has been acting kind of strange lately. I just thought he was stressed."

My smile grew with her doubt. "Maybe he's stressed because he doesn't want to get caught."

"Do you know something? Did you see something you're not telling me?" The color drained from Elizabeth's face.

"I don't know anything. But I wouldn't be surprised if he was seeing a younger woman. I hear that's what guys like. The younger, the better. Or so I hear."

"Did you see him with someone?" She brushed a tear away from her eye. "You can tell me."

I shook my head. "I didn't see anything. You should just be careful." I reached for the remote sitting between us and changed the channel.

"Is everything okay with you? I feel like I don't even know you anymore."

"I'm fine," I snapped as I flipped through the channels. "I hate that you have to keep asking me that. Why can't people just leave me alone? I'm fine."

"I'm sorry. I worry about you. I know how hard it is to be a teenager, and then will all your..."

"My what? What are you trying to say? You think you're better than me, don't you? It's no wonder Richard has a girlfriend. It's not like you're any prize." I threw the remote and stood up.

"This is what I'm talking about. You never acted like this before." Elizabeth sniffled. "I want to make sure you have everything you need."

"What part of I'm fine, don't you understand? Jesus."

"I'm sorry." Elizabeth reached down and picked up the remote.

"Would you shut the fuck up?" I mumbled under my breath as I made my way back to my room. What was it going to take to get that bitch out of my life? She was the only thing standing in the way of my true happiness.

CHAPTER FIVE

Five minutes into the school day and I couldn't bear to listen to the teacher drone on about god knew what. I took my backpack and made my way to the bathroom, the one farthest from class so Mr. Dean couldn't send someone to find me. When I swung open the door, Bertha was sitting on the side of the sink.

"Hey, look what the cat dragged in." Bertha took a drag off her cigarette. "How do I have the pleasure of seeing you again?"

"I was looking for someplace quiet. Looks like you were, too." I rested against the wall, unsure of my next move.

"Well, looks like you've come to the right place." Bertha spread her arms out before putting the cigarette in her mouth.

"What are you doing here? Don't you have class?" I

took a step away from the wall and set my bag down to sit on it.

"Does it look like I care?" Bertha tossed her head back and laughed. "Besides, I knew you'd be here." She winked.

"You did? How?"

"I knew you weren't like all the others as soon as I met you. You're different. Not one of those stuck-up preppy bitches." Bertha flicked the ash on the floor.

I flipped my hair and peered up at her. "You think I'm different?"

"Not is a weird way. Jesus, calm down." Bertha laughed. "Don't make me change my mind about you."

"It's just that..." I hung my head.

"It's that bitch, isn't it?" Bertha extinguished the butt in the sink before washing it down the drain.

"It is, but you wouldn't know her." I twirled my pant leg around my finger.

"No? I bet I have a good idea." Bertha put her fingers to her chin and raised her brow. "It's that bitch you live with." She looked up at me. "I'm right, aren't I?"

"You are. How'd you know?"

"I know things; it's what I do." Bertha shrugged. "That's not all, though, is it?"

I shook my head. "How do you know me so well?"

"I've been there before." Bertha lit another cigarette and handed it to me. "Want one?"

"No, thanks."

"You don't smoke?" Bertha took a puff. "Good, don't start. It's a bitch to quit."

"So I've heard." I watched Bertha as she sat on the sink and looked away from me, fascinated by her insight.

"You're a little freaked out right now, aren't you?" Bertha nodded.

Nervous laughter filled the space between us. "A little, I guess."

"Ah, don't be. I'm harmless." Bertha walked over to me and held out her hand to pull me up. "Come on, let's get out of this place."

"I don't know if that's a good idea. I'm already in so much trouble for skipping school. I think I should stay." My hand fell to my side when Bertha let go.

"For real?" Bertha scratched her head. "I really thought you were different."

"I am." I scanned the room and swallowed all of my apprehension. "Let's go."

"That's my girl." Bertha winked and took my hand. I followed her out the front door. "Where should we go? It's a great day for some trouble." She laughed and tugged on my hand.

"How about down by the river? It's usually quiet down there this time of day."

"Alright, that should do." Bertha rubbed her hands together. "Did you bring anything to drink?"

"No." I thought back to the bottle of vodka I had found earlier, wishing now that I had kept it.

"Well, that's a shame." Bertha reached for my hand. "Looks like we'll just have to make our own fun."

The walk to the river felt quicker than usual, almost like I drifted there. I took the scenery in as memories flashed back to me. I closed my eyes to push them out.

"This place is getting to you, huh?" Bertha sat on the grass facing the water. "It will get better." She tossed a stone in.

"How do you know so much about me?" I sat next to her on the tall grass.

"I don't. I'm good at guessing." She put a blade of grass between her lips.

"Really? You're that good?" I threw a rock into the river, watching the water splash up around it.

"What else do you think? You think I'm inside your head or something?" Bertha laughed. "Look, I'm as messed up as you are. I've got my own story to tell."

"Tell me." I picked at the grass underneath me, creating a pile between us. "I want to know as much about you as you know about me."

"Nah, I'm not one for storytelling." Bertha looked over at me and smiled. "I know you like to talk. Tell me your story."

"My story? What do you mean?" I cleared my throat and swallowed the growing lump.

"You know what I mean. Tell me about Elizabeth. What she does to you." Bertha's eyes locked with mine.

"I know I didn't tell you her name. How'd you know?"

"You told me. Don't you remember? In the bathroom. You must have been too upset to remember." Bertha reached into her pocket and pulled out her pack of cigarettes. "I'm listening."

"She's a bitch. I hate her. She's always getting into my business." I gazed out into the water. "She wants to see me fail. She always has."

"It sucks when people can't leave well enough alone, doesn't it?"

"It does. Life would be perfect without her. I could be with Richard, and we'd be happy. She doesn't want me there. I know it."

"Do you want her there?" Bertha took a drag and blew out a cloud of smoke.

"No." Thinking about Elizabeth fueled the dormant anger resting inside of me. "She should get the hell out. She should let me live my life. Richard and I would be happier. She's the problem, not me."

"Keep going. Tell me what you wish would happen." Bertha nodded and smiled. "Go on."

"If Elizabeth would just go," I threw a large rock into the water, "I'd be happy. She's why I hate my life. She's evil."

"That's right. She's the devil. The devil that is in your way."

"She is!" I balled my fist and punched it into the ground. "The devil needs to die."

"She does, doesn't she? The devil needs to die. Die, devil, die." Bertha smiled and tilted her head. "Die."

I stood up and clenched my fists. "I fucking hate her!" I screamed so loud, my throat burned. "Die, devil, die."

"That's it." Bertha got to her feet and clapped. "Die, devil, die. Die, devil, die." She chanted to the rhythm of her clapping.

My body swayed to Bertha's song. She was right. It was the only way to get the life I wanted. Elizabeth would have to die.

CHAPTER SIX

Lost in a daydream of how life was going to be, the sound of the bell made me jump out of my skin. "Hey, are you going to sit there all day?" Marcus gave me a nudge.

"No, I was just thinking." I grabbed my bag and stood up. "Well, are you going to move out of my way?"

"I was hoping you'd come out to the parking lot with me." Marcus put his hand in his pocket. "And, you know."

"No, Marcus, I don't know." I put my hand on his chest and pushed him out of my way.

"Come on, you know you want to." He took a step back.

"I'm not into you, Marcus. You just don't do it for me."

"That's not what you were saying the other day." He reached for his phone.

"Put that thing away. I don't care what you think happened, but I don't like you. You're not my type."

"If you don't come out there with me, I'll show everyone the video." Marcus scrolled through his phone before holding it up. "There, look. It sure looks like you were into me."

Laughter bellowed from my lungs. "Go ahead and show people. If you really want them to see that poor excuse for a dick."

Marcus turned the phone off and put it in his back pocket. "You're such a bitch, you know that?"

"I'm aware." I grinned as I walked out of the classroom, leaving him to stew in his misery alone.

When I arrived at English class, I saw the back of Kendra's head. She was just the person I needed to talk to. I slid into the chair next to her and tapped her on the shoulder. "You wouldn't believe what Marcus just did."

"Send out a porn video you two took?" She raised her eyebrows.

"He sent it?" I slammed my fist on the desk. "That sonofabitch."

Kendra rolled her eyes. "Why would you let him film it? It's gross."

"I didn't know he was filming it, and I didn't even know I did it."

"You don't remember doing it?" Kendra's eyes widened.

"No, not at all. I don't know how he took that video."

I pulled my book out of my bag and flipped through the pages.

"People have been talking." Kendra looked around the room.

"What do you mean? People have been talking about me?" I pointed to my chest.

She nodded. "Marcus isn't the only guy you've been fooling around with."

My face flushed. I closed my eyes, not sure how to come clean with her. I knew how much she didn't want Kevin and me to be together. "Like who?"

"Benny, Eric, Todd...I don't know. There's a long list. I figured it was just gossip. I didn't actually think there was anything behind it, not until I saw the video." Kendra flipped over her phone. "Have you been messing around with all of them?"

"What? No, of course not. I have no idea why they're saying that stuff. I hate them all." I tapped my book on the side of my desk, trying to pull up some memory. "I honestly don't know what they're talking about. I don't understand why you don't believe me."

"You've got to admit, it's pretty hard to deny it when there's evidence." Kendra opened her book and peered down at the pages. "Kevin got the video, too."

"Kevin? As in your brother?" I bit my fingernail. "Why would he get it? He doesn't even go here anymore."

"I don't know. The real question is, why does he care so much?" Kendra avoided eye contact.

"I don't know, Kendra. I don't know why everyone is trying to ruin my life."

"Looks like you're doing a good job all on your own." Kendra shrugged, her gaze focused on the pages in front of her.

"Kendra, why are you doing this to me? I thought you were my best friend." My eyes stung with betrayal.

"Yeah, me too."

I blinked the tears away and tossed my book into my bag. A bottle of vodka stared back at me. Without another thought, I raced to the bathroom at the end of the hall. There was something inside me that needed to empty that bottle. It needed to wash away the despair gnawing a hole in my stomach. As soon as the door shut behind me, I twisted the cap off and put the bottle to my lips. With one long chug, I poured the putrid liquid down my throat.

"What, you're not going to share?" Bertha jumped off the sink and walked toward me.

"Oh, sorry, I didn't see you there." I wiped my mouth on my sleeve.

"Rough day?" Bertha crossed her arms.

"You can say that again." In the mirror, I didn't recognize myself. Who was I becoming?

"Was it the devil?" Bertha stood behind me.

"Not this time." With my hands cupped together, I splashed cold water on my face. "I hate it here."

"Well, let's get out of here." Bertha smiled and reached for my hand.

"I really can't leave again. I need to graduate so I can get the hell out of here. I don't want to ever come back."

"Ah, who cares? You don't need to graduate. It's only a piece of paper." Bertha rubbed her hands together.

"I hate everyone." I slapped my reflection in the mirror. "I hate everyone!"

"Whoa, calm down." Bertha reached for my hand. "Come on, let's go."

I took her hand and followed her out of the building. The light from the hall felt like we were walking into a tunnel. "Where are we going?"

"Does it really matter? Let's just get as far away from this place as we can." She pulled me down the sidewalk and into an open field. I ran behind her to keep up. When I reached her, there was a path in front of us. She motioned for me to follow.

"What is this place?" I looked around and saw the river—the same one we were at on the other side of town. "Wait…"

Bertha put her finger to her lips. "Shh, it's our little secret." She sat on the ground and patted the grass next to her.

"How is this possible?" I spun around to take it all in. "How are we already here?"

Bertha's shoulders lifted. "Don't ask questions."

"And how do you know how to get here when you're new here?"

"I said don't ask questions." Bertha shook her head.

"Do you want to figure shit out, or do you want to play twenty questions?"

I sat next to her, holding my legs to my chest. "I don't understand."

"You don't have to. That's the beauty of it." Bertha smiled. "So, tell me about your day. What made it suck?"

"Oh my god, did you see the video?"

"The one with you and Marcus?" Bertha turned to look at me.

I covered my face. "I guess that's a yes."

"So, what's the big deal? It's not a crime to get laid." Bertha took the pack of cigarettes out of her pocket.

"The big deal is I don't remember it. I don't remember doing any of that stuff with him. And now Kendra told me other guys are saying they did the same stuff with me." I rested my head on my knees.

"They're liars." Bertha blew out a circle of smoke.

"But you saw the video."

"But you didn't do it. I believe you."

"How can you? I don't even believe me." I sighed. "How does Marcus have a video if it didn't happen? I saw it. It was me with him."

"Well, you've got two choices." Bertha took a long drag. "One, he photoshopped the whole thing, or two, he raped you."

"Oh my god, what if you're right? What if they all did? What if everyone is out to get me?" My heart raced at the thought.

"You have to be one step ahead."

"What do you mean?" I folded my legs under me.

"You've got to figure out a way to turn their world upside down. Make them pay for what they did to you." Bertha tossed her cigarette into the water.

"How do I do that?"

"You grab them by the balls and squeeze." Bertha snickered.

"That's your big plan?" I rolled on the grass and laughed. "You want me to go up to them and grab their dick?"

"It could work, but I wasn't being literal. I mean, you find their soft spot and expose it. Do any of these pieces of shit have a girlfriend?"

"I don't think so, at least no one from our school."

"Okay, how about a job?"

"I think Marcus works at the grocery store. Why?"

"Make a complaint. Get him fired. You've got to think of what's going to hurt the most and do a little more. Push the knife in and give it a twist."

"I like that option." I rubbed my hands together.

"Oh, so you want to really hurt them?" Bertha wiggled her eyebrows. "I like how you think."

"I wouldn't really do that. I couldn't."

"You'd be surprised at what you can do when you want it bad enough." Bertha made a stabbing gesture and stuck out her tongue.

"I could do it to the devil." A smile spread across my face at the thought.

"Now, you're talking. A knife to the neck keeps the devil away."

"I don't know, though. I can't stand the sight of blood." A shiver traveled down my spine. "I wouldn't want it on me. Besides, I'd be sure to get caught if I had her blood all over me."

Bertha held her chin in her hand. "Unless you could get someone else to do it for you."

"Well, that's not a very good idea. They rat me out in a heartbeat. I can't get anyone else involved. You already know too much."

"Who am I going to tell? I only talk to you." Bertha laughed. "I could do it. I love a good crime scene."

"No, I want to do it myself." I laid back onto the grass and put my head on my folded arms as I looked up at the clouds. "I just have to find a way. The perfect murder."

CHAPTER SEVEN

With a frown on her face, Elizabeth passed the bowl of mashed potatoes. "Your school called. They said you left during third period again."

"And?" I pushed a leaf of lettuce into my mouth.

"And this is becoming a habit. Principal Whittemore said you're at risk of failing." Elizabeth dropped her shoulders. "What's going on?"

"I don't really care if I fail." I tilted my head and smiled. "Why do you?"

"You're close to the end. Why wouldn't you want to finish? You worked so hard the last few years. I'd hate to see you lose everything now." She looked down at her plate. "I think it's time for you to see the doctor."

"No, I'm not going. You can't make me."

"Yes, she can," Richard spoke up. "And she should."

"What the hell is your problem?" I glared at him through narrowed eyes.

"It's for your own good. You've been acting strange lately. I don't think it would hurt." Richard pushed a forkful of potatoes into his mouth.

"Maybe you should go to the doctors and get your limp dick looked at." I pushed my plate across the table and tipped my chair over.

"That's enough." Elizabeth stood up.

"Let her go." Richard cleared his throat. "You can try again tomorrow."

I spun around in the doorway. "Funny, that's what you said last night, lover boy." I winked before I blew him a kiss.

"What is she talking about?" Elizabeth turned her attention to Richard.

"Yes, what am I talking about?" My finger tapped against my lips.

"Go to your goddamn room." Richard banged his fist on the table.

"Or is it your room?" I smirked before I stormed out of the kitchen. My door slammed so hard, the mirror fell off my wall. "You can both go to fucking hell!"

I threw myself onto my bed and turned the music on. *You Don't Know How It Feels* shook the speakers on my desk. I nodded my head to the melody and took out my phone. I had five missed calls from Kevin but not one message from Kendra.

"Hey." I hit send and waited for Kevin to reply.

The vibration of the phone ringing jolted my hand. I stared at the screen before answering. Why wouldn't he simply text me back? "Hello?"

"Where have you been? Or should I say, who have you been with?"

"It's not what it looks like. I can explain." I turned the music down and sat on the edge of my bed. I closed my eyes and took a deep breath while I searched for the right words. The idea of not knowing gnawed a hole in my stomach.

"I don't want to hear your lame excuses. I saw you and Marcus with my own eyes. I—"

"I don't remember being with him."

"You don't remember? What the hell? Do you think I'm stupid?"

"No, I really can't remember. I think Marcus either drugged me or photoshopped the video."

"Photoshopped it? Are you for real?"

"You're not listening to me. I didn't want to be with him. I don't even like Marcus."

"It sure looked as if you like him." Kevin played the video over the phone. "Hear that? Sounds like you were enjoying yourself to me."

"Turn that off." Nausea rose to the surface as I heard the unrecognizable version of myself. "I'm telling you I didn't agree to whatever happened. I wasn't there of my own free will. I think he drugged and raped me."

"Knock it off. It didn't look like you were drugged or raped. It looked like you were a willing participant."

"Look, Kevin, I don't know what to tell you." I picked at a loose thread on my comforter. "You either believe me, or you don't."

"No, you don't have the right to turn this around on me."

"I'm not. All I'm saying is you either love me enough to believe me, or you don't. I'm telling you the truth. I did not willingly have sex with Marcus."

"What about the other guys? Did they rape you, too?"

"What are you talking about?" I leaned back on my bed and rubbed my forehead.

"Like five other guys are saying you fucked them, too." Kevin sniffled. "I thought you said I was your first. I thought you loved me."

"Kevin, I do love you." My throat closed at the sound of my words. "I swear to you I didn't do anything with Marcus or anyone else. I only want to be with you." I rolled my eyes.

"I want to believe you. I really do, but I don't know if I can. It feels like you're messing with me. Like you think I'm stupid or something."

"That's not it at all." I sat up and crossed my legs. "I want to know what's going on as much as you do."

"So, you really don't remember being with Marcus?" Kevin's voice cracked.

"No, I don't. I don't know what's happening to me. My friend Bertha told me I should make him pay for what he did to me."

"Bertha? Who the hell is Bertha?" Kevin snickered. "Sounds like she's an eighty-year-old or something."

"She's new. I met her the other day, but she's awesome. She seems to understand everything I'm going through."

"Why don't you talk to me? You know I'm always here for you, right?"

"I know, but sometimes I need to talk to another girl." I rubbed the bridge of my nose. "It's..."

"What about Kendra? Why don't you talk to her?"

"I do, but she's pissed off at me."

"Why's that? What happened?" Kevin asked.

"Because she seems to think I'm dating her older brother. She won't talk to me now. She thinks I'm a whore, too."

"I'm sure you're exaggerating. You guys are best friends; she'll get over it." Kevin cleared his throat. "I'm sorry I got her involved."

"It's fine. She didn't believe me either."

"I'm sorry. I'm glad you have your new friend."

"Yeah, me too. I've got a killer headache. I'm going to have to let you go."

"I love you. I'm sorry I was so upset."

"It's fine." I tossed the phone onto the floor and covered my head with my blanket. The room went dark, erasing all of the day's problems. Tomorrow was another day. Another problem.

CHAPTER EIGHT

Marcus was in the back of the store stocking shelves when I found him. I knocked a can onto the floor and stood back. He didn't react, so I pushed two more off the shelf. I crossed my arms and watched him pick the cans up. I kicked off the entire bottom row of beans and waited for him to pick them up.

"What the hell are you doing here?" Marcus looked around the isle. "You're going to get me fired."

"That's the plan." I smiled as five more cans got added to the mess.

"Knock it off." Marcus bent over to pick them up. I kicked the side of his head. He fell to the floor and put his hands over his ear. "What are you doing?"

"Trying to repay you for all the joy you've given me." My foot connected with his stomach. When I pulled my foot back, I aimed lower and kicked him in the balls. "Go fuck yourself, you little bitch."

Marcus laid curled up in the fetal position when I walked away. I turned back around and emptied the stack of cans he had been filling the shelves with. With a smile plastered on my face, I walked out of the store and down the road. I had no idea where I was going, but I had a feeling I needed to get out of sight before someone came looking for me. I scanned my surroundings before I took the path into the tall grass.

The path emptied into an open field, hidden by trees and bushes. I followed the field to the edge and found the river. The same one Bertha brought me to the other day and the same one from the other side of town. I walked down to the rocky riverbank and sat down. The water rippled around the stone I tossed in.

"Fancy seeing you here." Bertha's raspy voice made the hair on the back of my neck stand up.

"Holy shit! Where did you come from?" I pushed the hair out of my eyes.

Bertha shrugged. "The real question is, where did you come from? I was here first."

I nodded. "True." I glanced over my shoulder.

"Are you hiding out?" Bertha threw a rock into the water.

"Yeah, how'd you know?"

"You look like you've seen a ghost. And you keep looking behind you like you're expecting someone."

"It's that obvious, huh?" I stretched my arms out in front of me.

"Just a little." Bertha held out her pack of cigarettes. "Want one?"

"Nah, I don't smoke." I held my hand up.

"It'll calm your nerves." She pushed them toward me.

"No thanks. My nerves are fine." I laughed. "Marcus might need one."

"Oh, do tell." Bertha put the butt between her lips and turned her body to face mine.

"I did what you said. I went to his work to make him pay."

"What did you do?"

"I threw a bunch of cans on the floor, and then when he went to pick them up, I kicked the shit out of him." I clapped my hands. "I've never felt this good."

"Did you make him bleed?" Bertha raised her eyebrows.

"I don't think so. I didn't stick around to find out."

"Smart. You don't want to get in trouble for something like that. Not when you have bigger fish to fry."

"What do you mean?" I picked up a handful of stones and let them fall between my fingers.

"The devil."

"True." I lowered my head. "I guess I could have messed everything up."

"Nah, it's fine. It's a good first step." Bertha blew out

a cloud of smoke. "You showed that little bitch who's boss. I bet he'll never mess with you again."

"You don't think he'll call the cops, do you?" I brushed the dirt off my hands.

"If he does, all you have to do is tell them he raped you."

"But I'm not sure he did." I held my forehead. "I don't even know what really happened."

"It doesn't matter. You said you didn't want it. That's rape."

"The video looked like I wanted it. I wasn't telling him no. I never told him to stop." I closed my eyes to push back the tears.

"Your word against his. He's going to college, right?"

"I think so."

Bertha lifted her shoulders. "Then he's not going to want to mess around with this. He'll drop it. You've got him by the balls."

"I sure as hell kicked him there." I snorted. "I didn't want to stop. The harder I kicked him, the more I wanted to do it."

"That's a good sign." Bertha nodded. "You're almost ready to take care of the devil."

"I still don't know how to do it. As much as I wanted to see Marcus suffer, I'm not sure I could have stood to see his blood everywhere. At the moment, it was amazing, but..."

"It gets easier. Maybe you need some more practice."

ISABELLE

Bertha rubbed her cigarette butt into the ground before she flicked it into the water.

"How do I get practice killing someone without getting into trouble?"

"You don't kill them; you've just got to hone your skills. Get ready for the grand finale." Bertha clapped her hands together. "Boom."

"I don't have a gun. I don't even know how to use one." I leaned my head back. "It's useless, isn't it?"

"No, there are other ways to skin a cat."

"Gross." I stuck my tongue out. "I don't want to hurt anyone's pet."

"It's a figure of speech." Bertha snickered. "Maybe you need a little more time."

"But I need her gone. I need her out of my life."

"What's the hurry if you know the end result."

"She said she wants to bring me to the doctor." I picked up the biggest rock I could find and chucked it into the river.

"What's the big deal with that? Who cares?"

"I do. The last time she pulled this shit, they tried to make me take something. A goddamn horse pill. I hated how it made me feel. I gained a bunch of weight, and my head was always killing me."

"What was it for?" Bertha squinted her eyes.

"I don't know. I flushed them, and I told the bitch I'd never take anything ever again."

"Okay, so you need to make your move sooner than

later. Unless you can dump them again. It's not like she can force them down your throat."

"True, but I don't want to go. I hate when people get in my business." I pushed my legs out in front of me.

"How else could you get rid of her?" Bertha tilted her head.

"I don't know. Right now, it seems like Richard is on her side." I leaned back on my hands and sighed.

"Why do you think that?"

"Because he took Elizabeth's side the other night. It makes me want to kill him when he does shit like that. Why can't he just love me?"

"Hmm." Bertha tapped her finger to her lips. "I have a crazy idea."

"What is it?"

"Does Richard have any children?"

"No."

"Does he want any?" Bertha raised her brow.

"I don't know. He never said anything about it."

"What do you think would happen if he got you pregnant?"

I put my hand to my stomach. "I don't know. You think it could work?"

Bertha nodded. "He couldn't deny it, and when the devil found out, I bet she wouldn't stick around."

"You're right." I rested my hand on my belly and rubbed. "He'd have to pick me then. She couldn't even give him any kids, but I could."

"It's worth a shot. Either that or you take the shot." Bertha laughed. "You'll get a bang either way."

"Or I'll get both." I rocked on the ground as I imagined the plan taking shape. Being a mom didn't sound that bad. "You're a genius. It's a foolproof plan."

"Follow me grasshopper for more life advice." Bertha winked.

"You're the best friend I've ever had." I stood up to give her a hug.

She held her hands out. "No, I don't do that sort of thing. Be careful who you trust. It can get you into trouble."

CHAPTER NINE

I waited for Elizabeth to go to work before I left my room. Richard was at the table finishing his breakfast. I sat next to him and took his hand.

"What are you doing?" Richard looked over his glasses at me.

"I wanted to tell you I was sorry for the other night. I didn't mean anything I said."

He pulled his hand away. "You need to be more careful. You're going to get people talking. You know we can't have that."

"I know. I was mad. I won't let it happen again." I walked away from the table and went back to my room. I pulled out a box of condoms and pushed a pin through the packaging in a few places. When I was satisfied with the results, I went into my closet and took out the lingerie Richard had bought me to slip it on. I took the condom with me and returned to the kitchen.

I pushed Richard's plate away and sat on his lap. I placed his hands on my breast and kissed him. "Let me make it up to you." Richard moved my hair and kissed my neck. I took his hand and stood up. "Come with me."

"Where are we going?"

I picked the condom up from the table and led him to his room. I pushed him onto the bed and pulled off his shorts. "I want you to make love to me." I got on top of him and held his hands down while trying to sit on him.

He pushed me away. "Not without a condom." He leaned up to kiss me.

I opened the package in my hand and slid it on him before I got on top of him. There was no way he would be able to tell the condom was full of holes until it was too late. Either later today or nine months from now. When he was finished, I rolled off of him. I couldn't wipe the smile off my face. It was easier than I had anticipated. "Want to do it again?"

"You know I can't. Not yet." He rolled over and kissed me.

"How about tonight?" I nuzzled into him.

"If we can find some time to sneak away."

"I hate that we have to be so secretive." I pulled him closer.

"I know, but what we're doing is just between us. It's better this way. It's more exciting."

"It will be." I kissed his chest.

"What does that mean? Are you making promises?" Richard laughed. "I love it when you want me."

"Me too."

"You know I want you. I'd be crazy not to want someone as hot as you. It's complicated; that's all."

"Do you think we could ever have a life together?" I buried my head into his side.

"I don't know. Like I said, it's complicated. Let's just enjoy what we have right now and take things as they come. You never know what the future will bring. Why not have a little fun in the meantime?"

I pulled my head up to look at him. "Okay." I had him right where I wanted him. As long as I could get him to make love to me until I got pregnant, the plan would fall into place. It was only a matter of time before Elizabeth wouldn't be able to avoid the truth.

Richard pulled me into him. "I know you hate it when we ask you but is everything alright with you?"

"God, really? You want to talk about this now?"

"I care about you, and it seems like something is going on. I want to make sure you're okay."

"I'm fine." My body burned from embarrassment.

"I care about you. I only want what's best for you." Richard patted my shoulder. "You're a good kid. You have a bright future ahead of you."

"For fuck's sake. I hate when you call me a kid. You just fucked me. Do you make it a habit of fucking children?" I pulled the sheet over my naked body and rolled away from Richard.

"You know it's not like that. You know what I mean. I'm allowed to care about you."

"You can either fuck me or pretend to be my father, but you can't do both."

"Don't be so obscene. You know I'm not a pervert. Can't a guy want what's best for the people he loves?"

"People? My god, you should stop now." I pulled the sheet off the bed and covered up with it. "Make up your mind. It's her or me."

"Don't be such a child." Richard sat up. "If you want to be a grownup, you need to start behaving like one. This attitude you have lately is not something a lady would have. If you want me to even consider a life with you, you need to work on your shit."

"Well, if you can't take me as I am, maybe you should keep your dick away from me." I gritted my teeth as I watched my plan dissolve before my eyes.

Richard held up his hands. "See? This is exactly what I'm talking about. You need help."

"And you don't?" I shook my head. "You are such a hypocrite. I'm good enough to fuck, but you want to pull this crap? You can go fuck yourself."

"We can stop anytime. If you're not happy, we don't have to keep this up." Richard shrugged.

I closed my eyes and took a deep breath. "I'm sorry. You're right. I'll try to be better."

"That's more like it." Richard smiled. "I only want you to be happy."

"Yeah, me too."

"So, you'll go to the doctor?"

"Is that what you want me to do?" I tilted my head and pushed up a fake smile.

"I think it would make Elizabeth happy."

"Right, because that's all that matters." I nodded.

"Happy wife, happy life." Richard lifted his shoulders. "It won't be that bad."

"What if they find out about us?"

"What do you mean?" Richard stood up and stretched.

"Well, if they want to know what's bothering me, and I happen to tell them that I'm in love with a man I can't have."

"Don't tell them. Simple as that."

"But, if they really pry, it might slip out. We can't have that, can we? That wouldn't make for a happy wife or a happy life."

Richard pulled on his boxers. "Hmm."

"Think on it? I'd hate to mess all this up by going to the doctor. I'm fine. Isn't that, right?"

"The more I think about it, I think you're right. Let me see what I can do. I'll talk Elizabeth out of it."

"Perfect." Maybe my plan was better executed than I had thought. I might even be ready for the second half of the mission.

CHAPTER TEN

Marcus hadn't been in school since the incident at the grocery store. It didn't seem like anyone even noticed he was gone. Maybe I killed him. The thought stopped me in my tracks. I closed my eyes to pull back the memory of the attack. When I left, he was breathing and screaming like a little bitch.

The moment I opened my eyes, Kendra was standing in front of my desk with her hands on her hips. "Hey."

"Hi." I looked up at her, not knowing what to expect.

"Kevin told me to tell you I was sorry. He said I was being a lousy friend." She lifted her shoulders. "I'm sorry. I guess I overreacted."

"It's fine." I bent down to get my bag.

"He told me you have a new friend. So, maybe you

don't even want to be friends anymore." She took her seat next to me. "I'll understand."

"What are you doing?" I stood by my desk. "We've got to get to class."

"We are in class. What are you talking about?" Kendra frowned. "Have you been drinking again?"

"You know I don't drink." I looked around the room. She was correct; we were in English class.

"Yeah, sure." Kendra pulled out her book. "Are you alright?"

"I don't remember walking here. Last thing I recall, I was in History." I sat back down and pulled out my book. "I don't understand what is happening."

"Wait, so you don't remember walking here? That was literally like less than five minutes ago."

"Seriously, I don't remember." I blinked my eyes. "I'm scared. What's happening to me?"

"Are you messing with me so that I'll believe you about the Marcus thing?" Kendra turned to look at me. "Because that would be—"

"No, I'm not making this up. Last thing I remember, I was in Mr. Ford's room. I swear I'm not lying."

"And you haven't been drinking?"

"I told you, I don't drink." I closed my eyes to try to regain focus. "My head is starting to hurt."

"You're serious, aren't you?" Kendra leaned over and put her hand on my forehead. "You don't have a fever."

"I'm not sick." The bell rang, and Mr. Dean closed

the door. I took a deep breath to calm the anxiety swirling inside my stomach.

"Ms. Mullen, are you okay?" Mr. Dean walked down the aisle and stopped before he reached me. "You look rather pale."

"I don't feel good." I covered my mouth.

"Why don't you go see the nurse? None of us want to see that." Mr. Dean shook his finger. "Go on."

I took my backpack and headed for the door. I didn't want to go to the nurse. There was no way I was going to let her know what was happening. It was not like she could recover my memories. I walked past her office and went to the bathroom.

In the stall, I tried to get rid of the vomit burning my throat, but it wouldn't come. I sat on the toilet seat and covered my face. "What is happening to me?"

"It's nothing to worry about." Bertha's dark brown eye was peering through the opening of the stall.

I looked through my fingers. "How come you're always everywhere I am."

"What? You're not happy to see me?" Bertha shook the door. "Come on out, let's talk."

"No." I covered my eyes and sobbed. "I'm broken. There's something wrong with me."

"Stop it. You know that's not true. Has the devil been talking to you again?"

"It is true. I can't remember anything. I don't even know where I am. I'm a failure." I pulled my legs up onto the rim of the toilet seat and hid my head in my knees. "I just want to be alone."

Bertha climbed under the stall. "I'm not leaving you alone, not when you feel like this." She held out her hand. "Come on, let's talk."

I shook my head. "I don't want to."

"It's not good for the baby to be this upset."

I lifted my head. "Baby?"

"Yeah, you're pregnant, aren't you?" Bertha leaned against the closed door.

"It doesn't happen that soon, does it?" I wiped my nose on my sleeve.

"It could. You don't want to risk it over this, do you?" Bertha held her hand out. "Come on, let's get out of here."

"I can't skip today. It's not worth it." I took her hand and stood up.

Bertha nodded. "Okay, we can stay here." She led me out of the stall.

We sat on the floor by the sink. Bertha slid closer to me and held my hand. "I can't remember anything." My tears returned.

"It's okay; I can't either." Bertha shrugged.

"And I think I killed Marcus, but I can't remember exactly. I just know I haven't seen him since I kicked him in the balls."

"He's fine. He's just scared of people finding out he got his ass kicked by a girl."

"How do you know?" I blinked the tears out of my eyes.

"I paid him a visit. I told him to stop being a jackass and to leave you alone." Bertha laughed. "He doesn't dare run into either one of us."

"You really went to his house?"

"Yup. I didn't want him doing anything stupid." Bertha winked. "I may have kicked him in the nuts, too."

"Oh my god, you didn't." I snorted. "The poor guy will never be able to have kids."

"It's probably for the best. Douche bags like him don't deserve to have kids."

"And you really think I'm already pregnant." I rested my head on her shoulder.

"I think so. That's what happens when you want something bad enough." Bertha stroked my hair.

"I think I'm ready for phase two of the plan. I need to get rid of her before the baby comes. I don't want her to steal it from me."

"Kill the devil it is." Bertha draped her arm over me. "You're going to be so good at it."

"I hope you're right. I still don't know how I'm going to do it."

"You'll figure it out. Focus really hard on it, and it will come to you. Like a vision. You'll see it like a movie playing out in your mind." Bertha snapped her fingers. "And then you'll know."

I closed my eyes and let the video reel play. My

cheeks raised as my smile grew as the possibilities played out before me. "How will I know when I figure it out?"

"You won't be able to look away."

CHAPTER ELEVEN

A bottle of medication was on the kitchen counter next to the bowl of fresh fruit. I picked it up and read it. I set it back down when I didn't see my name printed on the label. I took out the tallest glass I could find and filled it with orange juice. This would have to do until I could get some prenatal vitamins. I didn't want them kicking around while Elizabeth was still alive.

"You found your medicine." Elizabeth poured a cup of coffee. "I wanted to talk with you about them before you started taking them."

"Those are not mine. You can't make me take someone else's pills. That's against the law." I took a drink before I set my glass down. "What the hell is wrong with you?"

"Honey, they are yours. I talked to your doctor and told her what's been going on. Since you refused to go see her, she thought it was best to at least get you started on the medication she prescribed last time. It might help you feel better."

"Are you deaf or just stupid?" I shook my head. "You have no idea what you're talking about. You're clearly delusional. Those are not my pills."

"They are yours. I thought you looked at the bottle." Elizabeth calmly took a drink of her coffee.

I took the bottle and opened it, dumping the contents in the sink. "There, are you happy now? They're all gone."

"Why would you do that? I only want to help you." Elizabeth reached for the empty container.

I threw it across the room. "If you want it bad enough, you can go get it."

Elizabeth began to cry. "Why do you have to be so mean? I love you."

"Like hell you do. You love making my life miserable. You love being a goddamn whore, but you don't love me. That's fucking evident."

"I didn't want to do this, but you leave me no option." Elizabeth picked up the phone.

"What the hell are you doing?"

"I'm calling the police. I can't do this anymore." Elizabeth started to dial the number.

I rushed over to her and pulled the phone out of her hand. "Why are you calling the cops on me? You just said you love me. You are such a fucking liar."

"Give me my phone back now." Elizabeth took a step closer to me. "Right now."

"Or what? What are you going to do about it?" I held the phone out of her reach.

"I'm afraid of you." Elizabeth headed for the front door.

"Where are you going?" I followed her, pulling on her shirt. "You're not going anywhere."

"You're scaring me. Let me go." Elizabeth squirmed under my grip.

"Why are you afraid of me? I wouldn't hurt you."

"You're hurting me now. Let me go."

"Only if you promise me, you won't call the police."

"Okay, I promise. Please, don't hurt me," she whimpered.

I let go of her shirt, and she ran out the door. "You fucking bitch, where do you think you're going?"

"Relax, I just need some air." Elizabeth bent down with her hands on her thighs. "I won't call."

"Good." I threw her phone on the ground by her feet.

Elizabeth reached down to pick it up. I rushed toward her. She held her hands up. "I'm not calling anyone. I swear."

"Why can't you leave me alone? Why do you have to play these games with me? I never do anything to you! Why do you want to hurt me so bad?" I paced the yard.

"I screwed up so much of your life. I don't want to hurt you anymore. I was trying to help. I want to see you succeed. You deserve that." Elizabeth took a step toward me.

"Stay away." I held my hands out in front of me. "What do you mean?"

"I know how hard the first few years of your life were. I don't want to see it ruin the rest of your life. I want to make it up to you. I thought that's what I was doing."

"I don't know what you're talking about. What are you saying?" I punched my open palm.

"Honey, if you don't remember, I'm not going to remind you." Elizabeth hung her head. "I wish I could forget."

"Forget what? Remember what? What are you talking about?" I pulled at my hair.

"This is why I wanted you to take those pills. They would help calm you down." She took a slow step closer to me. "Don't you want to feel better?"

"I feel fine. You have no idea what you're talking about. You just want to ruin me. You hate me."

"Oh, honey, that's not true at all. I love you so much." Elizabeth closed her eyes and held her chest. "I hate seeing you like this."

"Like what?" I screamed. "Like what?"

"Angry. Sad. Scared. Confused. I don't know, whatever it is that you're feeling. I want to take it all away from you."

"You make no sense. First, you want to poison me, then you want to have the cops take me away. And then you love me and want what's best?" My head felt like a volcano, ready to explode. The image of my brains coving Elizabeth like hot lava made me laugh.

Elizabeth tilted her head and looked at me. A smile spread across her face. "I do. That's all I want for you."

"Have you thought maybe you're the one who needs help? Not me? Why is it all on me to get fixed? You're the only one who sees a problem. Maybe it's you who should take the pills." I nodded as the words sunk in. "You should take the pills."

"I'm getting help. I have been for years. You've met my therapist, Rose. We had a session together a few years ago, remember?"

Another thing I couldn't recall. I shook my head to push out the uncertainty. "So, do you take medication?"

Elizabeth nodded. "I do. It has helped me a lot. It hasn't made me sick or gain weight or any of the bad things you hear about. At my last checkup, I got a clean bill of health."

"How many do you take?"

"One. That's all I wanted you to try, too. Start out slow to see how it works and go from there."

"Where do you keep your pills?" I folded my arms and smiled.

"In my room, but they're not the same ones the doctor thought you should take. You see, everyone is different. You can't take mine, just like I can't take yours. The wrong medication can make you sick. That's why we wanted you to restart what you had been used to."

"So, if I took your pills, I could get sick?" I raised my brow.

"That's right."

"And if you took my pills. You could get sick?"

"Correct." Elizabeth smiled. "So, do you want to give it a try? See how they make you feel?"

"I do." My smile matched hers as the movie reel played in my head.

CHAPTER TWELVE

"I've got it!" I swung open the bathroom door and looked around the room. No one was around. Defeated, I went into the stall and locked myself inside. "You're so stupid!" I hit my hand against my forehead.

"You're not being mean to yourself again, are you?" Bertha's voice pulled me out of the spiral of self-hatred.

"I was looking for you." I opened the stall door and gave Bertha a hug. "The movie played."

"The movie in your head?" Bertha tilted her head and looked down at me.

"Yeah, and it's going to be perfect."

"See, I told you it would come." Bertha pulled a cigarette out of the pack with her teeth and lit it. "So, tell me about it."

"I'm going to poison her with the pills she's trying to poison me with." I rubbed my hands together.

"Oh, that is perfect. Get the devil at her own games." Bertha took a drag and blew the smoke out.

"She's filling my new prescription, and as soon as I get the chance, I'm going to pour her a glass of juice and fill it with poison. She'll be dead, and I won't have a mess to clean up."

"Sounds like a pretty solid plan. What happens if she figures out what you did?" Bertha flicked her ashes on the floor.

"She won't. I'll be careful." I crossed my arms and leaned against the wall. "It's a foolproof plan. It has to work."

"Then it will." Bertha twisted her foot on the butt before she sat on the side of the sink. "The devil's days are numbered."

"I can't believe I didn't think of this sooner. I should never have dumped those pills in the sink." I lowered my head. "I could have already done it."

"Don't beat yourself up. It doesn't matter when it happens, only that it does, right?" Bertha's smile lit up her face.

"You know, I don't know what I would have done without you. You're like an angel or something."

"Or something." Bertha laughed.

"No, but really, you're the person I want to tell everything to. You're my best friend."

"Oh, stop it. You're going to make me blush." Bertha got on her feet and held her hand out to me. "So, do you want to go on an adventure today?"

"No, I can't." I frowned. "I've got to get back to class. Do you want to hang out after school?"

"Nah, I'm busting out of this joint early." Bertha took a cigarette out and placed it between her lips.

"Do you ever go to class?"

Bertha lifted her shoulders. "When I feel like it."

"What classes are you in? I've never seen you in any of mine." I followed her out the bathroom door.

"You know, the usual." Bertha headed for the front door. I stood in the hall and watched her leave. I wished I could live my life more like her. She was a free spirit. Never worried about anything.

When I got to class, Marcus was crouched down in his seat. I kicked his desk as I walked by to get to mine. "Long time no see." I snickered when he flinched.

"Leave me alone." Marcus cowered, hiding his face from me.

"Nah, I don't want to." I leaned over my desk to get closer to him. "Not until you're dead."

Marcus didn't turn to look at me. "Did you just threaten me?"

"Nope. That's a promise." I slammed my foot into the leg of his chair.

Marcus raised his hand. Mr. Ford's back was to us as he wrote on the whiteboard.

"What are you going to do, you little pussy? Tell on me?"

"Mr. Ford." Marcus's voice cracked. "Mr. Ford."

Mr. Ford turned around. "What is it, Marcus?"

"Can I please change seats?" Marcus reached down to get his backpack.

"Why do you need to do that?" Mr. Ford put his hands on his hips and peered over his glasses. "You really felt the need to disrupt my class for that?"

Marcus stood up and walked to the empty seat. "Sorry, I just can't sit there."

"That's absolutely absurd." Mr. Ford shook his head and threw his hands up. "But whatever it takes for you to shut up." Mr. Ford went back to writing on the board.

Marcus shriveled into his chair. He covered his face with his hand like he was trying to disappear. The more uncomfortable he looked, the more I wanted to antagonize him. I leaned back and smiled as I thought what Bertha would do.

I got up and walked over to Marcus and cuffed him in the back of the head before excusing myself to go to the bathroom. Marcus held his head and whimpered. The kids sitting near him held back their laughter, but I could tell they appreciated it as much as I did.

On my way to the bathroom, I saw the back of Elizabeth's head sitting in front of Principal Whittemore's desk. I spun around on my heels and walked into the office. "What are you doing here?" I focused my attention on Elizabeth, who was dabbing her eyes with a tissue.

"We were just about to page you to come down here to join us. Great timing, young lady." Principal Whittemore stood up and pointed to the chair next to Elizabeth.

"Why? What are you talking about?" I crossed my arms and scowled.

"Have a seat, and we can tell you what we've been discussing." Principal Whittemore continued to point to the empty chair.

I slid into the seat and crossed my arms. "So?" I turned to glare at Elizabeth.

"So, I was telling Principal Whittemore that you've been having a hard time." Elizabeth turned her attention to him and nodded.

"Yes, I mentioned we have noticed you've been struggling." Principal Whittemore folded his hands and smiled.

"No, I have not. I'm fine. Everything is fine." I dug my fingernails into the inside of my arm and smiled.

"It's okay to ask for help when you need it. We all have bad days." Principal Whittemore sat back in his chair. "You've changed a lot since you started at Crystal River High. You had so much drive. You were going places." He lowered his head and shook it. "You're not that same girl."

"People change. Why is this such a big deal? And why is she here? You think it's okay to talk about people who aren't even here?" My face turned up as I tried to bring the conversation back around. "I appreciate your concern, but I'm fine."

"I'm glad to hear it." Principal Whittemore opened a file on his desk. "Do you have a reason why you've missed school recently?"

"I'm bored." I shrugged. "It's too nice to be stuck in here all day when the sun is shining." I smiled. "I mean, whatever happened to senior skip day?"

"That's not really a thing. It's just something kids created. We do not authorize it, but we don't stop it." Principal Whittemore pointed at the paper in front of him. "But we're looking at senior skip semester. You've skipped far more than one day, or even one week."

"I've always been an overachiever." I laughed.

"You are at risk for failing your senior year." He looked up at me. "I wouldn't be doing my job if I didn't do something to intervene."

"I'll stay in school. Is that what you want?" I glanced over at Elizabeth, who was still staring straight ahead.

"Well, yes, that would be a great start. But after talking with Elizabeth, I'd like to also suggest the name of some therapists." Principal Whittemore closed the file.

"I'm not talking to anyone. I have friends I can talk to. I promise you there is nothing wrong. I will stay in class. What more do you want from me?" My fingernails went deeper into my arm as I tightened my grip.

"I'm glad you have friends. That's important. It's also important for you to be safe and for your family to be safe. Sometimes things get out of our control, and we do stuff we normally wouldn't. I know you're a good kid; you just need some help to pull you out of this funk you're in." Principal Whittemore folded his hands in front of him. "Elizabeth, do you have anything you'd like to add?"

Elizabeth cleared her throat. "I know you're eighteen, and you don't have to do what I ask you, but I think it would be very helpful for you to talk with someone. You used to have a good relationship with your therapist."

"Like I told you, I am fine. There is nothing wrong with me. I'm sorry if I'm not who you want me to be. People change. That's what life is all about. We're supposed to grow and experience new things. I don't understand what the problem is."

"You had such big dreams. Do you still?" Elizabeth dabbed her eyes with the ratty tissue.

"Yes." I smiled and looked back and forth between the two of them.

"I'm glad." Elizabeth sniffled.

"That's great to hear." Principal Whittemore pushed his glasses up. "Do you mind sharing with us what they are?"

"Sure. To get the hell out of here." A Cheshire cat grin spread across my face. "Are you happy?"

Principal Whittemore nodded. "I see you haven't lost your sense of humor."

Elizabeth sighed. "I don't know how to help you. I've tried. I don't know what else I could have done." She started to sob. "I'm sorry I let you down."

I rolled my eyes. "Don't be overly dramatic. There's nothing wrong with me. I'm fine. Kids skip school; it's normal. I don't know why you're making such a big deal out of this."

"There's more to this than skipping school." Principal Whittemore handed Elizabeth a box of tissues. "Your behaviors are out of character."

"What do you mean? My behaviors?" I raised my eyebrow, unsure if he knew about Marcus or which part if he did.

He cleared his throat as his cheeks turned red. "There's ah...um...been some videos circulating the school."

"Videos?" Knowing what he was talking about, I wanted to at least make him as uncomfortable as possible. "What do you mean?" I tilted my head, awaiting his response.

Principal Whittemore coughed into his hand. "Videos of an uncomplimentary style."

"I don't know what you mean. Uncomplimentary?"

"You know what he's talking about," Elizabeth spoke up. "You're becoming promiscuous."

"Are you calling me a whore?" I pointed at my chest. "You think I'm a slut?"

"No, I'm not saying that. But I did see the video, and I hear there are more." Elizabeth dropped her head. "Are you at least being safe?"

"Wow. You wanted to call me in here and tell me I need therapy, and then you have the audacity to call me a whore? Are you for real?"

"No one is calling you a whore." Principal Whittemore stretched his arm across the desk to straighten a picture frame. "We simply want to help. We don't want to sit back and watch you crash and burn."

"We? As in the two of you?" I glanced back and forth between the two of them. "So, you're a thing now?" I nodded. "Cool. I'm sure Richard would love to hear this."

"Stop these games. You know what he meant. You're impossible." Elizabeth covered her face.

"Oh god. Here we go." I slapped my leg and laughed. "Make sure you put on your best show."

"You see." Elizabeth pointed at me. "This is what I have to deal with."

"And there it is." I shook my head. "It's always all about you, isn't it? Have you ever thought that maybe you're the problem? Not me. You need serious help." I got up and stormed out of Principal Whittemore's office. I turned to go back to class but couldn't get myself to go. I let the front door close behind me, and I didn't look back. I needed to find Bertha now more than ever.

CHAPTER THIRTEEN

My heart raced with every step closer to where Bertha might be. My surroundings became a blur as my vision focused on my destination. When I arrived at the path to the field I had been drawn to days earlier, I increased my pace as I pushed the tall grass out of my way.

"Bertha! Bertha!" I cupped my hands and yelled as I ran toward the water.

"I knew you wouldn't be able to stay away." Bertha smirked as she took a drag of her cigarette. "Looks like you need one of these." She held her hand out to me.

I took the cigarette and put it to my lips, inhaling the smoke into my lungs.

"See, look at that. You're an old pro." Bertha reached behind her. "How about a drink?"

I took the bottle of beer and emptied it with one long

sip. I tossed the bottle to the ground. "I need another one."

Bertha nodded as she handed me the next one. "There's plenty where that came from." She winked as she held up a six-pack.

"How'd you know I'd need these?" I wiped my mouth on my arm and took a third.

"I just knew." She leaned against the oak tree and watched me drink. "It's the devil, isn't it?"

I nodded as I finished the third beer. "She's got to go. I can't wait for her to fill my prescription. She has to die now." I fell to my knees into the grass and pulled myself over to sit next to Bertha.

"What's your plan?" Bertha tilted her head.

"I don't know." I closed my eyes and held my head.

"What do you think would work? There's got to be another solution. When someone needs to die, there's always a way."

"I don't know." My body fell backward. When I opened my eyes, everything was twirling around me.

"Think. It will come to you." Bertha came over and laid next to me.

"I can't think straight." I closed my eyes to try to stop the spinning.

Bertha took my hand. "Have patience. It will come to you."

The blackness behind my eyes began to play a movie. "I can see it."

"Go on, tell me what you see." Bertha squeezed my hand.

"I'm in the bathroom at my house. The medicine cabinet is in front of me. I can see myself opening it."

"What do you see next?"

"There's medicine in there." My face turned up in a smile. "I'm taking out a bottle of some kind of pills."

"And then?"

"And then I'm in the kitchen, and I crush them up to put them in the devil's coffee." I sat up. "Oh my god, that could work. We have stuff at the house already that could work."

Bertha rubbed my back. "See, I knew you'd figure it out."

"You're so smart. I knew you'd have the answer."

Bertha shook her head. "I didn't do anything. You came up with it all by yourself."

"But I couldn't have done it without you."

"I'm flattered, but this was all you. You're smarter than you know. All you have to do is believe in yourself." Bertha folded her hands and placed them under her head.

I joined her in the grass. "I love you, Bertha."

"You shouldn't." She laughed. "I could be the devil, too. You can never be too careful."

"Oh, stop it. I know you're not. You're more like an angel. My guardian angel." I reached for her hand.

Bertha snorted. "That's brilliant." She shook her

head. "So, when you get home, you're going to do the deed?"

"With Richard?" I looked up into the sky. "It has been a while."

"No, you horny bastard." Bertha smacked my arm. "The deed. You know. Kill the devil. Then you can do the deed with Richard any time you want."

The image of me waking up wrapped in Richard's arms filled my mind. "Yeah, I'll do it as soon as I get home."

"That's my girl." Bertha looked over at me. "You're thinking about Richard right now, aren't you?"

"How'd you know?" I turned to her and smiled.

"It's all over your face. That's when you know you're doing the right thing. When something makes you this happy, it's got to be right."

"You're right. This is going to be way easier than I thought."

"What are you going to do with the body?" Bertha's question pulled me out of my bliss coma.

"The body?"

"Yeah, when the devil is dead, there'll be a body." Bertha pointed up at the sky. "Maybe you can get some of those crows to eat it."

"Eww, gross." I tried to shake away the visuals. "But, seriously, what do you do with a body?"

"You could bury it, burn it, chop it up, throw her into the river." Bertha shrugged. "Hell, there's all sorts of ways to get rid of a body."

"I don't want to do any of those things." I chewed my fingernail. "Why can't she just stay in the house until Richard calls the ambulance or something?"

"Ambulances don't come for dead people. And if he called someone, who's going to get blamed?"

"You're right." I sighed as my options dwindled away. "Do you really think they'd think it was me?"

"Everyone knows you don't like her. It'd probably be the first place they looked. And if you go to jail for murder, what's the point?" Bertha shrugged.

"Shit. I guess I didn't think this all the way through." I rubbed the bridge of my nose. "My head is killing me."

"Unless..." Bertha sat up and snapped her fingers.

"What? Unless what?"

"Unless you make it look like a suicide."

"How would I do that?" I sat up and pulled my legs to the side.

Bertha tapped her finger on her chin. "A note."

"She's not going to leave a note. There's no way I could get her to do that."

"Leave the empty bottle next to her. That way, it would look like she took them on her own." Bertha raised her brow. "Or maybe you just don't want it bad enough."

"That's not true. I want this more than anything." I blew out the breath I had been holding. "I'll figure it out."

Bertha nodded. "I know you will."

"I'll make sure the bottle is next to her body. That

would be the best thing. Then when Richard finds her, he'll find it." I clapped my hands. "Looks like I'm back in business."

"Perfect. I can't wait to hear all about it." Bertha's smile grew. "The devil is done."

CHAPTER FOURTEEN

The only thing I could use in the medicine cabinet was half a bottle of acetaminophen. I pulled it out and unscrewed the cap. A handful of pills fell into my hand. I put them back in the bottle and brought them to my room. At my desk, I took a piece of paper and spread the pills on top of it.

One by one, I crushed the pills by covering them with another sheet of paper and hammering them with the meat tenderizer I found in the kitchen. When each pill turned to dust, I poured it back into the bottle. When the pills were all crushed, I stuck the bottle into my pocket and went to find Elizabeth.

"Hey, I'm sorry about everything." I sat on the couch next to her.

She turned the TV off and sighed. "Okay, thank you for that."

"I know I have been impossible lately, and I want

you to know I'm ready to get help and do whatever it is you want me to do." I tilted my head and smiled. "I'm sorry."

"Alright." Elizabeth nodded. "You'll have to understand why I'm a little hesitant to believe you."

"I know. I haven't been very nice to you lately."

"No, you haven't, but I'm more concerned with how you've been treating yourself." Elizabeth lowered her head. "I understand why you'd be upset with me, but I don't want to see you destroy yourself."

I closed my eyes to regain my focus, pushing away the frustration brewing inside. "Understood."

"I'm sorry, too. I only want what's best for you, and if I've failed you, I'm sorry. I'll do whatever you need me to do to help get you through this."

"Thank you." I bit the inside of my cheek to keep myself from saying everything I wanted to.

"Do you think you're ready to get some help now?" Elizabeth put her hand on top of mine.

"I think so." My pulse throbbed in my neck as I tried to remain calm. "If it will make you happy, I'll do it."

"That's very sweet of you, but in order for it to work, you need to do it for you."

"I'll do it for me...and you." I blinked my eyes and smiled. "Whatever it takes."

"I'm so happy to hear this." Elizabeth leaned in to hug me. "I love you."

I moved closer to allow the hug. Everything inside me was screaming, but I had to play the part. I needed her to trust me. At least for a little while. "I love you, too."

Elizabeth rubbed her eyes. "You don't know how happy I am to hear you say that."

I smiled and sat back on my side of the couch. "Why don't we watch a movie or something."

"Oh, that would be lovely. It will be just like the old days." Elizabeth picked up the remote and flipped through the channels. "What made you change your mind?"

"I had a talk with a good friend."

"That's nice. It's so nice when you find those special people, isn't it? They can make everything better." She stopped on a Hallmark movie. "Look, it's one of our favorites."

"Great." I smiled through gritted teeth.

"Do you want me to make us a snack?" Elizabeth started to get up.

"No, let me." I held my hand out. "How about some popcorn?"

"That sounds lovely." Elizabeth settled back into her seat.

In the kitchen, I put a bag of microwave popcorn in the microwave. I looked over my shoulder and saw she was still in the living room. A new bottle of orange juice greeted me when I opened the fridge. I took it out and then went to the cupboard and took out two glasses. A clear glass and a tall, blue plastic cup.

The popping from the microwave drowned out the

noise from the living room. I looked behind me to see where Elizabeth was, and she still hadn't moved. I poured the juice into the cups and looked around the room again, making sure I was alone. My heart raced as I pulled the bottle of crushed pills out of my pocket.

The contents of the bottle floated on the top of the juice. With a spoon, I gave it a stir. The powder mixed into the liquid. The microwaved beeped, causing my body to jolt, spilling some of the drink.

"I'll be right there," I hollered into the living room. With the popcorn in a bowl, I placed it in the crook of my arm and grabbed the drinks.

"Oh, how nice." Elizabeth took her cup of juice, and I placed the bowl between us.

"I figured we'd get thirsty." I took a drink and waited for her to do the same.

"Great idea. Thank you." She placed her cup on the coffee table.

"You don't like orange juice?" I sat on the edge of my seat, looking between her and the cup of poison.

"I love it. I'm just not thirsty yet." She smiled and pulled her legs under her. "Why don't you get comfortable and enjoy the movie? It's been so long since I've seen this, it's like it's all new."

"Oh, that's great." I didn't pull my eyes away from her cup as I reached into the bowl and took a handful of popcorn.

"Is everything okay? Do you want to watch something else?" Elizabeth picked up the remote. "You probably don't want to watch this, do you?"

"No, it's fine." I sat back, letting my body sink into the cushions, and filled my mouth with our snack.

Elizabeth reached for her cup and took a drink. I watched and waited for her reaction. Nothing. She set the drink back down and went back to the movie. At least it didn't taste bad. I refocused my attention on the TV and watched the movie. I couldn't force her to drink it; she'd have to do it on her own time. The anticipation was going to get me before the pills got her.

The movie ended before Elizabeth finished her juice. It didn't appear she had drunk enough to do anything yet. Unsure what to do, I closed my eyes to pull up another plan. "Do you want to watch another movie?"

Elizabeth yawned. "I'm not sure I'll be able to stay up for another one." She stretched her arms over her head. "I've got to go to work in the morning, and you've got school." She stood up and picked up her cup.

"I guess you're right." I picked up the empty popcorn bowl. "You should at least finish your drink."

Elizabeth chuckled as she peered into the cup. "Sounds like something I would have said to you."

I shrugged. "It's a shame to waste good stuff."

"You're right." Elizabeth put the cup to her lips and took a sip. "Oh my, I think I let this sit around too long." She stuck out her tongue.

"Why? What's wrong with it?" I took a step closer to her to try to get a better look at the contents.

"Nothing's wrong with it. It's just a little warm." Elizabeth gave the cup a little shake.

"Maybe you should put it in the fridge and have it for breakfast." I pulled at my shirt to give me some air.

"It's really okay to dump it out. It's not that expensive."

"No." My voice was sharper than I had intended.

"Okay, if it'll make you feel better, I'll save it." She smiled as she walked into the kitchen. "It was really nice to spend some time together, just the two of us."

"Where's Richard? How come he's not home?" I hadn't noticed his absence until now.

"Oh, well, we're taking a little break." Elizabeth pushed my hair behind my ear.

"A break? What do you mean?" I put the dishes in the sink.

"Well, you remember our talk the other day? You told me you thought he might be fooling around on me. When I asked him, he didn't deny it. We both decided it would be best to take a little time away."

"What do you mean? You guys are splitting up?" I rubbed my forehead.

"It's nothing for you to worry about." Elizabeth smiled. "Everything will work out."

"I don't really think he's messing around on you. I was just being a jerk. You should call him and tell him you're sorry." I crossed my arms and bounced on my feet. "He should come home."

"It's really okay. I'm fine. I know you don't care for him. I should listen to you. You're what matters."

"No." I shook my head. "I shouldn't get involved in your life like that. You need to call him and get him to come home. Do you know where he is?"

"He's staying with one of his friends." Elizabeth dumped the juice into the sink and covered her mouth. "Oh shoot, I forgot to save it."

I rolled my neck and sighed. "Perfect," I muttered under my breath and headed for my room.

"Honey, I'm sorry. I didn't think you'd care. I know the two of you don't see eye to eye. I figured it would be better for all of us."

"Well, you obviously don't know me very well." I refrained from slamming my door and went to my bed. I grabbed a pillow and screamed into it. I didn't want all that work to go out the window. I had to come up with another plan, and fast. But first, I had to get Richard to come home.

CHAPTER FIFTEEN

When the bell rang, I went to the bathroom to look for Bertha instead of going to class. There was no way I could concentrate on anything except completing the plan. I searched around the room; Bertha wasn't in there. Like the other times, I waited for her to arrive. She always knew when I needed her. Today would be no exception.

The knock on the stall door woke me from my nap. "I knew you'd come."

"Who are you talking to?" The voice on the other side of the door was not Bertha's. I recognized it, though. Kendra pressed her face against the crack and peered in at me. "What are you doing in here?"

"What are you doing here?" I parroted the question back to her.

"I'm going to the bathroom. That's what people do

in here. Were you sleeping in here?" Kendra was still peering at me.

"I don't know. Maybe. Why does it matter?" I turned to block my face.

"Because it's weird. Why aren't you in class? How long have you been in here?"

"I don't know. I was waiting for someone."

"Who?" Kendra pulled on the door handle. "Come on, let me in."

"It doesn't matter. Just go to the bathroom and get back to class." I turned to see she was still staring at me through the opening.

"Is everything alright? You look like you've been crying."

"I'm fine. I was just waiting for someone." I got to my feet and opened the door. "I guess she isn't coming today."

"Who? Who are you waiting for?" Kendra put her hands on her hips. "Why don't you ever talk to me anymore?"

"It doesn't matter." I went to the sink to wash my hands.

"Yeah, it kind of does. We're supposed to be best friends. You used to tell me everything. Now, we never talk." Kendra frowned. "Did I do something wrong?"

I shook my head. "Bertha is different. She gets me."

"So, do I. Have you forgotten everything we've gone through together? We've been friends forever." Kendra crossed her arms. "I want to meet Bertha. I want to see what's so great about her."

"I don't think you two would get along." I laughed. "We're still friends; it's just that Bertha is helping me with something."

"Let me help you." Kendra took a step closer to me.

"It's not something you'd approve of. Don't worry about it." I put my hands up to separate us. "We can have other friends. We're not exclusive."

"I know that. I would like to meet Bertha. I haven't seen her around. You said she was new here, right? I'm sure she could use some more friends."

"Yeah, sure. When I find her, I'll tell her." I grabbed onto my backpack strap and smiled. "I'll see you around."

"Just wait for me to go pee. I want to come with you." Kendra went into the stall.

"No, I don't think it's a good idea. You shouldn't skip school."

"Ha, says you." Kendra flushed the toilet. "Wait for me. I'm coming with you." She washed her hands and followed me out the door.

"Are you sure you want to screw up your perfect attendance for this?" I held the door for her.

"Don't be a smartass. I'm not as perfect as you think." Kendra paused in the doorway.

"You don't have to come. I'll be fine."

"No, it just feels like I'm forgetting something." The door swung closed behind her. "Okay, let's go."

We walked out of the school together, and no one even noticed. "How is it that no one ever asks where we're going?"

"I don't know. They don't seem too bothered by it." Kendra shrugged. "Where are we going?"

"This way." I took her hand and pulled her in the direction of the path.

"Kevin said you've been avoiding him lately."

"What? Why would he say that? It's not like we're a thing." I picked up my pace, practically pulling her.

"You know I'm fine with it now. You guys can do what you want." Kendra tripped as she tried to keep up with me.

"Okay, whatever. Come on, it's just a little further."

"Where are we going, anyway?"

"To Crystal River. I know a shortcut." I let go of her hand and sprinted ahead.

"We're nowhere near the river. It's going to talk forever to get there." Kendra stopped to catch her breath. "Why don't we call Kevin to come pick us up?"

"No, it's fine. We're almost there."

"Seriously, we're not even close." Kendra pulled out her phone.

"Knock it off. I know what I'm doing. Come on." I went back and took her hand.

"Okay, if you say so."

"It's not that much further." I searched the side of the road. Nothing looked familiar. "It's here somewhere."

"What are you looking for?"

"The path to the river. I know it's here. I was here the other day." I dropped her hand and turned around.

"Is this where you come when you skip school?" Kendra pushed the hair out of her face.

"Yeah. This is where Bertha and I hang out. I really need to talk to her." I scratched my head. "I don't understand where the path went."

Kendra pointed behind me. "Is that it, over there?"

I turned around to look. "Maybe. Let's go check."

Kendra followed. "Is it?"

I stepped into the clearing on the side of the road. "I don't know. It doesn't seem the same." After a few more feet in, I knew it wasn't. "We've got to keep looking."

"Or we could just get a ride to the river. It's going to take forever to walk there."

"But it doesn't. It's usually right around here someplace. I don't understand what's happening."

"How'd you find this shortcut?" Kendra followed close behind.

"Bertha showed me."

"But isn't Bertha new here? How would she know about shortcuts like that?" Kendra put her hand on my shoulder. "Let's stop and think this through."

I pushed her off me. "No, I know it's here. I know we'll find it. I was surprised the first time, too. We've got to keep looking."

"Are we on the right side of the road?" Kendra put her hands on her hips and blew out her breath.

"I'm lost, not stupid. I know the river wouldn't be over there. It has to be on this side. Why don't you go back to school? I know you think this is dumb."

"I don't think you're stupid, but there's no way we can be that close to the river. It's miles from here. We've lived here our whole life, and I've never found this magic path Bertha showed you."

"Magic? Why are you being a bitch?" I blew the hair out of my eyes.

"You know what I mean. But think about it, how does it make sense?" Kendra's voice softened. "Were you drinking when you were there?"

"Why does that matter?" I rolled my eyes. "Just say it. Say you think I'm full of shit."

"I'm not going to say that. Let's call Kevin and see if he can take us." She took her phone out of her pocket and sent her brother a text.

"Fine, I guess it's the only way we're going to get there today." I looked up and down the road, trying to see where I went wrong. Everything looked different.

"He's on his way. He'll be here in less than five minutes." Kendra slipped the phone back in her pocket.

"That's going to be awkward." I twisted my foot on the gravel.

"What is? Seeing Kevin? He misses you." Kendra winked. "After trying to keep you two apart, you guys do make a cute couple."

"Can we not talk about that right now? I've got a lot on my mind."

"Talk to me. What's going on? What are you running from?" Kendra took my hand. "You know you can trust me."

"This is too much. I can't tell you what's going on. If you knew, you could get in trouble, too. I don't want that."

"But Bertha knows? How come it's okay for her to get in trouble, but not me?" Kendra wiped the sweat off her brow. "You can tell me anything."

"I don't think I can. This is big."

"I can handle it. We've solved a lot of problems together. What's one more?"

"This is way more serious than anything we've ever done." I closed my eyes to make her stop asking me questions. "Please, just trust me."

"Look, I can tell that whatever's going on is upsetting you. I want to help. You don't have to tell me details if you don't want, but at least let me help you." Kendra put her hand on my back. "You don't have to do this alone."

With my hand on top of hers, I smiled. "Thanks for the offer, but I think I'll pass. It's not personal. You'll thank me later. Trust me."

"Okay, fine. I'll drop it. Know the offer is there if you change your mind." Kendra took her phone out again. "Kevin should be here any minute."

"Do you think he's going to come to the river with us, or will he leave?"

"My guess is that he's going to drop us off. I doubt he'll be up for hanging out with his annoying little sister." Kendra giggled. "But he'd probably kill to hang out with you."

I turned my head. "Kill?"

"You know what I mean. He misses you." She held her finger to her lips. "He'll kill me if he knows I told you."

Kevin pulled up next to us. "Get in before anyone comes." He stared straight ahead, avoiding eye contact. Kendra reached for the backdoor. I pushed her hand away and got into the back. Kendra joined Kevin in the front. Seeing Kevin made me question everything. Memories of the time we'd spent together made me crave his skin next to mine. There was too much at stake to let my desires derail the plan. I bit my bottom lip as my body ached for his touch.

"So, you guys are going to Crystal River?" Kevin turned the radio up as he waited for the answer.

"Yup," Kendra yelled over the music. "Why would you turn that crap up right after you asked me a question?"

"If you don't like how I do things, you can walk." He reached over and turned the knob some more. "How's that? Better?"

"You're such a jackass." Kendra turned to look at me. "I don't know what you see in him."

Kevin reached over and hit her arm. "Don't be a jerk."

"Ouch." Kendra shrunk down in her seat.

Music was the only sound in the car for the rest of

the ride. Kevin pulled into the parking lot, but he still hadn't looked at me. "When do you need a ride home?" He turned his gaze to Kendra.

She turned to me. "How long do you think we'll be?"

I shrugged? "An hour maybe."

"Come get us in an hour." Kendra got out of the car and leaned in the window to say something to Kevin. I couldn't make out what she said, but it was the first thing that made Kevin smile.

I took Kendra's hand and started for the water. "Thanks for doing the talking. That was awkward."

"Ah, it wasn't that bad. He doesn't want you to know how much he misses you. He's trying to act all tough. You know how guys are."

I nodded. Except I didn't know. Guys were confusing. The thought of Richard with another woman made my blood boil. It was bad enough he was with Elizabeth, but to think of someone else in the way was almost too much to handle. "Bertha should be here. She's always here."

"Okay." Kendra smiled. "I'm looking forward to meeting her. She sounds like a great friend."

"She is." When we got to the clearing, I stopped and glanced around. "Hmm, I don't see her." I took a few steps closer to the water. "Bertha?"

"Are you sure she's here? Maybe she's still at school." Kendra stood beside me. "It doesn't look like anyone's here."

"She has to be. She wasn't at school." I stood on a

rock in the water and looked around. I cupped my hand over my eyes to block the sun. "Where is she?"

"I don't know. I mean, she could be anywhere."

"No, she has to be here." I slipped on the wet rocks and fell into the water. "Bertha."

Kendra jumped into the shallow water and reached for my hand. "Come on, she's not here."

"Bertha!" On my hands and knees in the water, I splashed around until I could stand. "Bertha, come on. I need you."

"I don't think she's here." Kendra reached her hand out again. "Come on, we can look somewhere else. Crystal River is a big place; she could be in town."

I shook my head. "She's got to be here. She always is." I got to the riverbank and pulled myself to the grass. "I don't understand why she's not here. She knew I would need to talk to her about what I did."

"What did you do?" Kendra crouched down next to me. "Tell me. I'm here. I'll listen."

"No, she's supposed to be here. She needs to help me figure something else out. She knew I would need her." I buried my head into my knees and rocked my body as I sobbed.

Kendra rubbed my back. "It's okay. We'll find her. Don't worry."

Kendra had no idea the magnitude of the need. There was no way I could figure out another plan without her. It was Bertha who helped the ideas come.

ISABELLE

When I closed my eyes without her, it was only blackness. The movie didn't play without her. With so much at stake, what was I going to do now?

CHAPTER SIXTEEN

The cramps were almost too much to take. I rolled over in bed and clutched my stomach. "Fuck." As with all the other plans, this one went out the window, too. At least Richard was back home now, so we could try again. But Elizabeth was still here, too. In a fetal position, I tried to squeeze the pain out of me, pressing my knees into my arms.

"It's time to get up." Elizabeth knocked on my door before she opened it. "What's the matter?" She came to my bed. "Are you alright?"

"No. I'm having bad cramps. I don't think I can even get out of bed." I whimpered through the pain.

Elizabeth got on her knees and put her hand on my forehead. "You're burning up. Let me get you some Tylenol. I'll call the school, too."

The pain, almost too much to bear, shot through my body. It wasn't good enough that my period was here reminding me of my failure, but it brought the most excruciating pain I had ever felt.

"We're all out of pain meds. I'll see if Richard can run to the store before he goes to work. I'll stay home with you, too." Elizabeth walked back to my bedside. "Can I get you anything?"

"Go to work. I'll be fine. It's only my period. I'm not dying." I pushed her away.

"I don't like how you look. I think I should stay home to be sure you're okay." Elizabeth stood in the doorway. "I wouldn't be able to live with myself if something happened to you."

"Don't be dramatic. I'll be fine. No one has ever died from period cramps. God." I clenched my teeth through the pain.

"I don't know, honey. This looks bad. Maybe I should take you to the emergency room."

"Fuck." I leaned into the pain. "It's just like you to use this against me."

"I'm not doing that. I want to make sure you're okay. It could be something else. Is there any way you could be pregnant?"

"What? No. How can I be pregnant if I'm having my period?" I swatted at her. "Go on, I'm fine."

"I'm going to call the doctor to be safe. You've never had cramps like this before." Elizabeth disappeared, and the pain intensified. "On a scale of one to ten, how bad is your pain?" Elizabeth returned with the phone to her ear.

"Fifty."

"She said fifty." Elizabeth paused as she listed. "Okay, alright. We'll be there as soon as we can." She turned the phone off. "They want to see you as soon as possible. Come on, let's go." She reached her hand out. "I can help you up."

"I don't want to go."

"The doctor said it could be something serious. It shouldn't take long. Don't you want to feel better?"

"Will they give me something for the pain?" I looked up at Elizabeth as the plan played out through the pain.

"I don't know. If you need them, they will."

I held my stomach as I pulled myself up. "Fine, let's go."

Elizabeth helped me into her car. Richard was already gone. I was glad he didn't have to see me like this. I rested my head against the seat and closed my eyes. The pain was worse now that I was upright. Elizabeth reached over and rubbed my knee. "I'm glad you decided to go."

"I don't really have a choice. This pain is crazy." I pulled my knees up onto the seat to push the pain back.

At the hospital, Elizabeth parked in front of the main entrance. "Wait here, and I'll get you a wheelchair."

"That's not necessary." A wave of pain shot through me.

"Don't be difficult." Elizabeth rushed into the hospital and returned with a nurse and a wheelchair.

ISABELLE

With both of their help, I was out of the car and in the chair. "Go ahead and park your car. We'll get her right in." The nurse wheeled me in.

When Elizabeth arrived, I was already in a bed, waiting to see the doctor. "Wow, they work fast here. What did I miss?" Elizabeth pushed the curtain out of the way to enter the room.

"They made me pee in a cup." I shrugged. "So, not much."

"That's good. What are they checking for?" Elizabeth crossed her arms as she paced the tiny room.

"What do you think?" I shook my head. "I'm not on my period." I fed her the lie I wanted to believe.

"Do you think you're pregnant?" Elizabeth pushed a frown off her face. "Don't worry. We'll figure it out."

"I guess we'll find out." The anticipation grew as we waited for the results. There was still a chance I was carrying Richard's baby. The pain was almost tolerable with that as a possibility.

"If you are, it can't be good that you're in all this pain." Elizabeth chewed on her finger as she walked circles in the room. "Where are they?"

The curtain pushed open. "Don't worry, ladies, the test was negative."

My heart sank. I clutched my stomach. "I need something for the pain." If that plan wasn't going to work, there was no way I was going to miss out on the opportunity for the other one to fall apart.

"I'll have the nurse give you something." The doctor

stood over me, his stethoscope hanging over his neck. He pressed on my side. "Does this hurt?"

Instincts kicked in, and I slapped him. "Get your hands off me."

He held his hands up. "If she's going to assault me, I'm not going to work on her. You can take her somewhere else."

"I'm not assaulting you. Keep your hands off me, and you'll be fine."

"If you want me to help you, I have to check you over." The doctor walked back to the side of my bed. "Will you at least let me see what might be wrong?"

I nodded as I remembered I needed to cooperate to leave with the pain medication. "What do you think it is?"

"I don't know yet." He pushed on my side. "Does this hurt?"

"Yes." I gritted my teeth and sucked in air.

He continued to feel around before he went to the sink and washed his hands. "It appears you have kidney stones."

"What does that mean?" I held my belly.

"It means it's going to hurt like hell." He coughed to cover his laugh. "I'll send you home with some pain medication, and you'll want to drink lots of fluid. Get plenty of rest, and you should be as good as new."

"That's it? That's all that's going to make the pain go away?" I turned to look at him. He was already out of the room.

He turned around and stuck his head back in. "Yup. It's going to hurt until you pass it. Could be today, could be tomorrow, or next week." He shrugged. "Just do what I said, and you'll be fine."

The pain meds had kicked in before we left. Elizabeth stopped at the pharmacy to fill my prescription. She handed me the bag. The answer to all my problems was now in my possession. Maybe I didn't need Bertha after all.

CHAPTER SEVENTEEN

"Where's Elizabeth?" I twirled my hair and stood in front of the TV.

"She's working." Richard set the newspaper down. "She's working a double to make up for the hours she took off yesterday." He patted the cushion next to him. "Why don't you come join me."

"Why don't we go to your room?" I pulled off my shirt and started walking away.

"It'd be more fun to do it out here." Richard took his pants off and stood in the doorway. "Come back here." He slid his boxers off.

I unhooked my bra and walked back to him. I pressed my skin against his and kissed him. "I have an idea." I nibbled on his ear.

"What is it?" Richard ran his fingers over my shoulders.

"Why don't we have something to drink. It'll be fun." I pulled his hand toward the kitchen.

"Okay." He followed me to the kitchen. "Do you even drink?" He raised his brow.

"A couple of times." I stood behind him and kissed his back as he poured us our drinks. He handed me a glass of wine.

"You like this stuff?" I took a small drink.

"Not really, but it will do." He emptied his glass before I had a chance to take another sip.

"Why don't you have something you like?"

"You're right." He opened the cabinet and poured a glass of whiskey. I watched as he drank it, still holding my glass of wine. "Why don't you have another?"

He nodded. "That's not a bad idea. It's been a while since I've had a few drinks."

I took a small sip of mine and watched as he finished his. I dumped the rest of my drink in the sink and took his hand. "Let's go to the bedroom."

He followed, no more mention of staying in the living room. I pushed him onto the bed and straddled him. He leaned up to kiss me, and I knew I could make my move. I slid onto him, not giving him a chance to use a condom. He didn't seem to remember, and when he finished, he gave me another kiss. Looks like I might have had a backup plan if I couldn't get Elizabeth to take my medication.

"I wish we could do this more often." Richard pushed the hair out of my face.

"Me too."

"If only Elizabeth were out of the picture, then life could be perfect."

"I know." I gave him a kiss before I rolled off and lay next to him. He held me close before he started snoring. The temptation to stay in bed with him and let Elizabeth find us was strong. The only thing stopping me was knowing it would get Richard kicked out. Without knowing where he was, there was no way of making sure he was mine.

I left him in the bed and went to the living room to pick up the mess we left. There was now no trace of what we had done. The bottle of pain medication from the hospital was on the counter. I grabbed the bottle and took it to my room. I crushed the pills, just like I had done before and returned their dust to the bottle, and hid it in my dresser.

I got into bed and closed my eyes. "Think." I needed the perfect plan to get this to work. The orange juice didn't work. The options of what would mask the taste were sparse. Coffee. My eyes shot open. I'd have to slip it into her coffee in the morning. I rolled over to try to get some sleep. I'd need to get up before Elizabeth to make the coffee for her.

My phone rang just as I was drifting off to sleep. I reached over on my nightstand to grab it. "Hello?"

"Hey, it's Kendra. I just heard some awful news."

"What's wrong?"

"Kevin told me he's moving out west."

"What? Why would he do that?" I blinked the sleep out of my eyes.

"He said he came by your place tonight to talk and..."

"And?" My heart flew into my throat.

"And he saw you with another guy."

Fear took my breath away. "He...he did what?"

"He said he saw you making out with some other guy."

"That's impossible." I squeezed my eyes closed.

"That's what I told him. Aren't your mom and Richard home?"

"She's not my mom." I sighed. "You know that."

"Sorry. But they're home, right?"

"Richard is. Elizabeth is at work." I sat up and rubbed my forehead.

"Oh my god." Kendra gasped. "You weren't...were you?"

"Weren't what?"

"You know. You weren't messing around with Richard. You hate him, right?"

"I don't know what Kevin told you he saw, but he's mistaken. You really called to wake me up to tell me this?"

"You were, weren't you? That's why you needed to see Bertha the other day, isn't it? You didn't want me to know about this." Kendra's breath was the only thing coming through the phone.

"You're mistaken. Why would you even think that?

This is why Bertha is my new best friend, and you're not."

"You told me you hated Richard. You said he hurt you. So, which is it? Oh my god! I can't believe Kevin saw you guys together." Her disgust radiated through the receiver.

"I don't know why you think I hate Richard. I never said that. But I wasn't doing anything with him." I rolled my eyes. "Why was Kevin snooping around my house anyway?"

"He wanted to apologize for acting weird the other day. He loves you. I guess he was trying to fix things."

"I have a phone. Why wouldn't he just call me?"

"I don't know. Does Elizabeth know you and Richard are fooling around? Is that even a thing? I mean, he's old enough to be your dad. Is this consensual? Is he hurting you? Because Kevin said it looked like you were into it. But I mean—"

I cut her off. "Would you stop? You have no idea what you're talking about. Richard and I were not doing anything. I don't know what Kevin saw, but it's not what he told you. Maybe he was seeing things."

"It seems strange that you're so defensive, especially after everything you've told me before about him. I should call the police, shouldn't I?"

"Why would you do that? Why do you want to ruin my life?" I pulled at my hair. "My god. This is why we're not friends anymore."

"I was trying to be a friend. A real friend would try

to make sure you're okay. They wouldn't let someone take advantage of you or hurt you. If you like messing around with an old man, go for it. Real friends give a shit; they don't let you think what you're doing is okay. But what do I know? You know what? I need to go see how my brother is doing. Go back to doing whatever you were doing. If you need me, you know where to find me." The phone went dead.

If Kendra called the police, it could mess up everything. Richard wouldn't get in trouble, not with them, but with Elizabeth. Why couldn't people mind their own business? I wished I had Bertha's number. I could really use her right now. Back in bed, I closed my eyes and tried to get rid of all of the chaos floating around. It was only a matter of time now.

CHAPTER EIGHTEEN

Elizabeth was still sleeping when I left for school. Luckily, I hadn't mixed her coffee yet. It would have to wait until tomorrow. After the accusations from Kendra, there was no way I was going to be able to face her. I grabbed my backpack and headed for the river.

I walked past the school to find the path. The one I couldn't find when I was with Kendra. After about ten minutes, the clearing on the side of the road presented itself. I knew it was here. I walked through the long grass, and when I got to the open field, I started to run. It had been too long since I'd seen Bertha.

As soon as I arrived at the water, Bertha was sitting on the bank, smoking a cigarette. "Hey, I knew you couldn't stay away."

"Where have you been? I've been looking for you." I caught my breath and sat next to her.

"I've been around." She shrugged. "Maybe you weren't looking hard enough."

"No, I spent hours trying to find you." I reached for her cigarette.

"Well, I was right here." She tossed the butt into the water.

"Hey, I wanted that."

"Life sucks sometimes, doesn't it? We can't always get what we want." Bertha tossed a rock into the grass. "Sometimes, we just don't try hard enough."

"What are you talking about? Are you mad at me?" I pulled up a handful of grass and threw it.

Bertha stared straight ahead. "Where's the devil?" She turned her head to look at me, her eyes wide.

"She's still alive. I tried, but it didn't work." I lowered my head. "But I have another plan."

Bertha held up her hand and touched each one of her fingers. "How many before you run out completely? Four? Five? A hundred?"

"Why are you mad? Why do you care if she's dead? You don't even know her."

"She's the devil. Everyone knows the devil. You're not the only person she's hurting. Why are you so selfish?"

"I don't understand. Why are you being like this?" I bit the inside of my cheek. "Why are you upset with me?"

"I know where Richard went the other night." She

winked. "I know why you want him so bad." Bertha licked her lips. "Mmm. He's a fine piece of meat."

"What?" My mouth dropped open. "Richard was with you? You—"

"Rode him like a pony." She waved her hand above her head. "Yeehaw!"

"Why would you—"

"You don't want him badly enough." Bertha shrugged. "He's fair game."

"Why are you being like this? You were my best friend." I blinked away the tears.

"Don't be so dramatic. You just met me. How can we be best friends? It doesn't work like that. You don't even know me." Bertha stood up and towered over me. "Maybe I'm the devil."

"You're not, though. I know you're not." I looked up at her, unsure what my next move should be.

"I hear Kevin got a little show last night." She tossed her head back and cackled.

"How do you know about that?"

"I told Kevin he should go to your place and fix things. He's a sad sucker. He really loved you. You really screwed things up."

"You know Kevin? How?" I got to my feet. Even standing up, Bertha still felt bigger than me.

"You don't own him, or anyone else for that matter. Kendra?" She laughed. "She's next on my list."

"Why are you trying to destroy me?"

"Me, destroy you?" Bertha shook her head. "Nope,

sorry, that's all on you. You did that all on your own. Accelerate it? Maybe."

"What did I do? I still don't understand what I did to upset you." I started to walk away.

"The problem is, you'll never know. You don't want to know. You're too busy hiding from yourself. You don't have time for anything else."

"That's not true. I came here special to see you. I have time for you." I turned back around. "I thought we could talk."

"You don't get it." Bertha shook her head.

"What?"

"What do you know about me?"

I paused as I thought back to our time together. "You just moved here and—"

"Did I just move here?" Bertha tilted her head. "Or did you find me when you needed someone?"

"You smoke."

Bertha clapped. "Okay, captain obvious. What else?"

"I don't know," I snapped.

"That's right. You don't know anything about me. But I know everything about you." She took a step closer and poked her finger into my chest. "I know where you live. I know who your friends are. I know who you're in love with. I know you want to kill the devil. I even know how you plan on doing it."

"That doesn't mean anything. All that proves is I'm

the one who does all the talking. It's not my fault you don't share anything with me."

"You are so thick-headed, you'll never get it." Bertha lit a cigarette. "You have until tomorrow night to kill the devil." She blew smoke into my face.

"Or what?" I took a step back.

"Or I call the cops and tell them everything." She held up her phone. "Better yet, I let you tell them everything."

My heart dropped to the pit of my stomach. "Why are you doing this?"

"I'm not doing anything. You are. You either kill the devil, or I go to the police." She turned and walked away. "The choice is yours."

CHAPTER NINETEEN

I stayed up all night to make sure I was awake before Elizabeth. I couldn't take the chance. There would be no way to explain away any of our conversations. I had said too many things that I couldn't take back. I tried to remember everything we talked about, but it was all already a blur.

I didn't know why Bertha was so desperate for me to kill Elizabeth. Unless. I closed my eyes as I pictured her and Richard together. Was she making me do her dirty work? Did Bertha want me to kill her so she didn't have to? She never mentioned that she was going to; she only encouraged me to.

The whole plan shattered to pieces before I had a chance to open my eyes. "Fucking bitch." Fury burned inside of me. I should have killed *her*. I shook the thoughts out of my head. "No. I have to do this." I got to my feet and paced my room. The sun would be up soon, and then Elizabeth. Bertha wasn't going to bully me out of my plan or into hers. Elizabeth would die, and Richard would be mine. End of story.

I found the bottle of crushed-up pills and put it in my sweatshirt pocket. I hadn't even bothered to get undressed last night. I didn't want to do anything to risk missing my opportunity. Richard wouldn't want Bertha anyway. And if I'm pregnant, he'd have to choose me. A smile spread across my face. This would work. It had to.

I opened my bedroom door and tiptoed to Elizabeth and Richard's room. I heard Richard's snoring and knew I still had a little time. By tomorrow night, it would be me in that bed next to him. The thought propelled me to the kitchen.

In the kitchen, I took out the coffee grounds and scooped them into the filter. I filled the coffee pot with water and poured it into the back of the machine. The sun was already starting to come up. My time was quickly running out. In the cabinet, I found Elizabeth's favorite mug and set it on the counter. A quick peek over my shoulder proved the coast to be clear. I took the pill bottle out of my sweatshirt and poured it into the cup. Panic set in when the coffee was not brewing fast enough.

I took out the creamer and poured a little into the mug. With a spoon, I stirred the contents. The powder disappeared. There was enough coffee in the pot to fill Elizabeth's mug. With just a little spill, I was able to fill her cup and return the pot. The deed was almost over.

ISABELLE

I set the coffee on the table where Elizabeth sat and paced the kitchen. Where was she? I looked down the hall. Their door was still closed. A package of cinnamon raisin bread was on the counter. I put two slices into the toaster, hoping the aroma would be enough to bring Elizabeth to the kitchen.

The toast popped out of the toaster, and there was still no sign of her. My pulse beat against my neck as time began to run out. If her coffee got too cold, she'd dump it and start over. I took out the butter and fixed her breakfast, placing it by her coffee.

The creek of her door opening brought back my hope. There was still time for this to work. I poured myself a cup of coffee and sat at the table. "Good morning, sleepyhead."

Elizabeth rubbed her eyes. "What is this?"

"I made you breakfast." I smiled as I held my mug between my hands.

"You did? Why?" She pulled out her chair and sat down. "This smells lovely." She took a bite of toast. "Perfect, just the way I like it."

"I fixed your coffee, too. Cream only?" I took a drink and waited for her to try it.

"I'm surprised you remembered." She took a drink and nodded. "Just the right amount of cream."

"Oh, good. I'm glad you like it." I watched as she finished her toast, barely touching her coffee. My gaze fixated on her mug.

"Thank you. This was a nice surprise." She stood up.

"What's wrong with your coffee? Is it too strong? Too much cream?"

"No, it's perfect. I like to drink it slowly as I wake up." She turned to look at the microwave clock. "You should get going before you're late for school."

"It's almost the end of the year. Who cares?" I shrugged. "Besides, I want to finish my cup."

Elizabeth shook her head. "No, I'm sorry. You've got to get to school. Take it with you if you want, but Principal Whittemore already had a fit about you missing the other day."

"Fine." I poured my coffee into the sink. "You'll drink yours?"

Elizabeth took another drink. "I will. Thank you, honey. Have a good day."

I hated that I had to leave before she finished her coffee, but if I stayed, she might suspect something. I could only hope it would work out. There was no other option. At the end of the driveway, I wasn't sure which way to turn. School or Crystal River were my options, and neither was where I wanted to be.

I took out my phone to call Kevin when I remembered he was upset with me. Kendra would be at school, and she most likely wasn't talking to me anymore. My circle seemed to keep getting smaller. I didn't have any friends. The only person I had was Richard, and I'd have to walk past Elizabeth to get to him.

In the middle of the sidewalk, I held my arms out and spun in circles. When I stopped, I started walking.

I'd go wherever the road took me. I'd only have to keep busy for a couple of hours before I could return to the house.

A car pulled up behind me. I kept walking. There was no way I was going to get in with a stranger. "Would you just get in?" The familiar voice stopped me in my tracks.

"Kevin? Why are you here?" I leaned over to peered in.

"Do you want a ride or not?"

I opened the car door and got in. "I thought you hated me." I buckled my seatbelt.

"Why would I be mad at you?" Kevin glanced over at me before turning his attention back on the road.

"Because Kendra said..."

Kevin scrunched up his face. "What did Kendra say?"

"You're not mad at me?" I reached over and rubbed his leg.

"I'm not mad. I thought you were mad at me." Kevin put his hand on top of mine.

"Why would I be mad at you?"

"I don't know. Because you haven't been answering my calls or texts."

"Sorry, I've been busy. There's a lot going on." I looked out my window. "Where are we going?"

"Crystal River. Isn't that where you were headed?"

"No. I'm not sure where I was going. I didn't want to go to school or the river. Not today, anyway."

"Why are you spending so much time there? What's down there?" Kevin put his directional signal on.

"I had a friend I was hanging out with." I squeezed my eyes closed. "Turns out she wasn't really my friend."

Kevin parked his car in the back of the grocery store parking lot, the same one Marcus worked at. "You and Bertha aren't friends anymore?"

"No. I'm sorry she bothered you." I looked at Kevin.

He shook his head. "She hasn't bothered me. I don't even know who she is."

"So, she didn't talk to you the other day?"

"No. I've never talked to her. Never seen her. I was starting to think you made her up to avoid me." Kevin leaned back in his seat.

"Why would I do that?" I rubbed his leg. "I like spending time with you."

He nodded. "Sure, you do. It's okay; I get it. I knew when we started dating it was going to be hard. I guess that's what I get dating my little sister's best friend."

"We're not friends anymore, either." I looked down. "Seems I don't have any friends."

"Stop that." Kevin sat up and took my hands. "You have me." He kissed the top of my hand.

"You have to say that because you want to get into my pants." I laughed and leaned over to kiss him.

"That helps, but I mean it. I care about you. I always will."

"I doubt it." I pulled away and sat back. "I'm sure you'll be sick of me eventually."

"That's not true. I'll always be here for you. No matter what. I know things have been hard for you at home."

"How do you know?" I squinted to block the sun.

"You told me." Kevin tilted his head. "Do you not remember our last conversation?"

"Yeah, of course, I do. I'm just stressed out, I guess. There's a lot going on with the end of the school year and stuff." I shrugged. "So, tell me what you've been up to."

"I found an apartment." Kevin smiled. "If I get approved, I can move in July first."

"An apartment? Wow, I didn't even know you were moving out."

"Yes, you did. I told you about it. We even drove by the place, and I pointed it out to you. It's the one on Maple Street. The old yellow Victorian."

"Oh, yeah, that's right." I nodded. "I can't wait to see it."

"I was thinking, maybe you'd want to move in. That is unless you're going away to school or something."

"You want to move in with me?" I pushed the hair behind my ear.

"Why wouldn't I? I love you. I want to spend my life with you." Kevin took his phone out and scrolled through his pictures. "Look." He handed me his phone. "This is the place."

"Oh, yeah, I remember now." I handed his phone back to him.

He pointed to an empty room. "This is where we could put the nursery."

"Nursery?" My face flushed.

"Yeah, when we get married and have kids. You said that's what you wanted."

"That's right." I smiled. "Sorry, my head hurts. I'm having a hard time thinking straight."

"Are you okay? Do you want a drink of water or something?" Kevin brushed his hand on my cheek.

"Sure, that would be nice."

"I'll be right back. Do you want anything else?" Kevin got out of his car and leaned in to look at me.

"No, that's it. Thanks." I settled into the seat and rubbed my head. I watched Kevin walk into the store and heard the sirens. An ambulance sped past the store. I turned to watch where it went. It disappeared out of sight, but the siren blew loud enough for me to hear it long after it was gone. My cheeks turned up so high, my eyes squinted. Until I remembered. Ambulances don't help dead people. Their job is to keep people alive. I punched my fist into my leg and gritted my teeth. "Fuck."

"What was that?" Kevin handed me a cold bottle of water as he got into the car.

"Nothing." I forced a smile.

"You looked like you were upset. Is everything alright?"

"Time will tell."

CHAPTER TWENTY

Kevin drove past my house to get to his. Elizabeth's car was gone. The ambulance hadn't been for her. Richard wasn't there either. I put my hand on Kevin's leg. "Let's go fool around." At this point, he was my only option.

"Really? You're up for that?" Kevin tightened his grip on the steering wheel.

"Why wouldn't I be?" My hand traveled up to his inner thigh.

Kevin squirmed in his seat. "Because we weren't really talking a few days ago. You know I want more from you than this, right?"

I blew out my frustrations. "Yeah, I know." I looked out the window and saw a car wrapped around a tree. "Slow down." I pressed my head to the glass.

"Oh man, that looks terrible." Kevin's eyes widened. "That's not…"

"It's Elizabeth's car." I bit the inside of my cheek to hide my excitement. "You should stop."

"I don't think that's a good idea." Kevin pulled his car over to the side of the road. "It looks like the ambulance is all packed up. Why don't we go to the hospital?"

"I need to see what happened." I unbuckled my seatbelt.

Kevin reached for my hand. "No, I don't think that's a good idea. Not yet anyway. Let's get to the hospital."

"No, I want to go over there." I opened my door and ran to the wreckage.

"Miss! Miss, you can't go over there." An overweight police officer held his hands out.

"I know her. I need to see—"

"Miss, she's on her way to the hospital. They'll fill you in. There's nothing to see here."

"Is she going to make it?" I bent down and put my hands on my legs to catch my breath.

The police officer frowned. "It's not my place to say, Miss. It doesn't look good, though. If I were you, I'd get to the hospital sooner than later."

I stood on my tippytoes to peer over the officer's shoulder. "Yeah, yeah, okay." I turned to walk back to Kevin.

"Sorry about your friend." The police officer took off his hat and bowed his head.

"Thanks." I waved before I got into the car. "He said we should go to the hospital."

Kevin nodded. "Alright." He held out his hand. "I'm sorry. I'm sure she'll be okay."

"I don't know. He said it was pretty bad." My heart raced with the anticipation. I fought to keep the smile off my face.

Kevin pulled into the closest parking space. I jumped out of the car before he had it in park. "Wait up. I'm coming." He shut his door and jogged to catch up with me. "Slow down."

"Hurry up." I didn't look back. I focused my attention on the front entrance. The automatic door opened at sloth speed. "Come on. Jesus!"

Once Kevin was by my side, he reached for my hand. "It's going to be okay."

I pushed him away from me. When the door opened, Richard was standing at the desk, tears streaming down his face. "How? How'd you find out?"

"Where is she? Is she going to make it?" I scanned the area.

Richard came closer and hugged me. "I don't know. They won't tell me anything."

"Is she still alive?" I pulled out of his embrace.

Kevin put his hand on my shoulder. "Give them some time."

I pushed him off. "No. I need to know now. Why can't they tell us if she's going to die or not? Why is it so goddamn hard?"

"Whoa." Kevin held his hands up. "Why don't we go get some fresh air."

"No, I'm not going anywhere until I know she's dead."

"You mean until you know she's alright?" Kevin took my hand. "Come on, let's at least go sit down."

Richard stayed at the desk when Kevin and I went to the waiting room. We sat in the back row, away from the rest of the people. "I don't understand what's taking so long. She's either dead, or she's not. Is it really that hard to figure out?" My body shook as every unknown crashed around me.

"I know you're upset, but you should watch what you're saying." Kevin put his hand on my arm. "Just take a deep breath and be patient."

I nodded. I needed to be careful. I couldn't let anyone see how eager I was to know, especially if it was because of me she was here. "You're right. I guess I'm nervous."

"I know." He gave my hand a squeeze. "All we can do is pray for her."

I bowed my head and wished for my desired outcome. The only one that would work for me. It would take Elizabeth's life to get the one I wanted. I closed my eyes and rocked in my chair, blocking out everything around me.

I felt Kevin's hand on my back. When I looked up, Richard was next to us. His hand was over his mouth. He shook his head and sobbed. "She didn't make it."

The news gave me a level of energy I had never

experienced. Everything I wanted was mine. I closed my eyes to hide my excitement. Silence swirled around as a blanket of darkness fell over me.

FIND OUT WHAT HAPPENS NEXT IN CRYSTAL RIVER

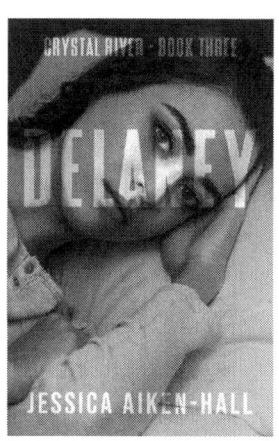

Delaney (Crystal River Book Three)

A novella that will keep you on the edge of your seat!

Falling asleep shouldn't be such a terrifying thing.

I woke up with blood on my hands, but no idea how it got there. The only logical thought is that I did something I should cover my tracks for. When I open my eyes again, I'm strapped to a bed at Crystal River Psychiatric Hospital.

My freedom is on the line as I struggle to put the pieces together and defend my sanity. No one seems to have any answers, and even I'm having a hard time believing the story that is unraveling. I have no one to turn to, no one to help prove my innocence. It's now up to me to uncover a secret life I don't even know about.

ABOUT THE AUTHOR

Jessica Aiken-Hall, author of her award-winning memoir, *The Monster That Ate My Mommy* lives in New Hampshire with her husband, three children, and three dogs. She is a survivor of child abuse and domestic violence and is a fierce advocate. Her mission is to help others share their story.

She has a master's degree in Mental Health Counseling, with over a decade of experience as a social worker. She is also a Reiki Master and focuses her attention on healing.

When she is not writing, she enjoys listening to Tom Petty, walking along the beach, looking at the moon, and watching murder shows.

To follow what she's doing next check out http://www.jessicaaikenhall.com.

Made in the USA
Middletown, DE
01 October 2021